Tomas

A Time Travel Romance
Dunskey Castle Book 3

Jane Stain

ISBN-13: 9781521164655

DEDICATION

To Scott

I love you.

ACKNOWLEDGMENTS

Thank you
Jimmye and Heidi
and Linda and Sondra
for beta reading and thus helping to
make Tomas the best book it could be.

Contents

(Chapter names are Gaelic numbers)

Aon (1)

Before she started looking for her friends, Amber went out through the terminal past the security checkpoint where everyone was waiting in line to get in. She'd never been to Scotland before, and the back of her mind was making plans just in case Kelsey and Tavish weren't there. She knew she was going out to the dig at Dunskey Castle. She could put her carry-on over her shoulder and roll both suitcases behind her out to the street, where there were always taxis waiting. The fare would be exorbitant, but she could get there okay. If she needed to.

She was looking at the overhead TV screens for which way to turn to go get her baggage when she heard Kelsey's voice.

"Amber, you made it!"

Breathing a small sigh of relief, she turned and smiled as first Kelsey and then Tavish gave her big hugs.

And then Amber pointed and laughed at Tavish as animatedly as she could.

"You aren't fooling anyone, you know. Modern day Scots wear modern kilts if they wear them at all, not old fashioned great kilts like your Renaissance Faire costume. And while our faire accent might sound authentic for a sixteenth century Scot speaking English, it doesn't sound at all like a modern-day Scot's English. I would know, because I just sat next to a whole Scottish family for six hours." She nodded to where the couple and their six and nine-year-olds were collecting their luggage.

The woman smiled and waved, and Amber waved back, making funny faces at the kids, who giggled.

Tavish flounced in his kilt as only he could, striking several manly poses and making even said modern-day Scots tsk at him playfully. Then with a teasing look on his face, he pointed at Amber's black Goth lipstick, big swinging skull earrings, lacy long black dress, pointy black shoes, and white make-up over olive skin.

"Well, you aren't fooling anyone either, you know. Modern day Goths are still in their graves, not out and about looking like The Walking Dead."

After she made a big show of rolling her eyes at Tavish, Amber told him and Kelsey about her

8

flight while they helped her gather up her bags from the carousel and take them out to their rental car. Tavish drove them a short distance to a pub he said was a great place to have lunch, to which Kelsey gave an exaggerated shrug.

But once the waitress had seated them and taken their orders, Amber asked her old friends the question that was on her mind.

"So how's Tomas?"

There, that was the part she really wanted to know. Well, actually, it was whether Tomas missed her. Did he ever talk about her? What did he say? Did they think the two of them would ever get back together?

But she'd settled for the tamer version. Oh, and better ask about the rest of their old gang as well. You know, so she didn't sound so desperate.

"And have you heard from your four favorite cousins or any of their girlfriends?"

Kelsey turned to Tavish and raised her eyebrow.

He smiled at Amber while he toyed with Kelsey's hand.

"I think I've finally convinced Tomas to come visit me here. You wouldn't believe how hard I've been trying, nor how long it's been since I've seen my twin."

Amber knew it was more important for Tavish to be in touch with Tomas than for her to be. Of course it was. Blood was thicker than all the spit she and Tomas used to swap. But her old boyfriend — and Tavish — had simply disappeared off the face of the earth seven years ago. And while Kelsey had explained briefly that the guys had separated from their girlfriends out of urgent necessity, Amber still didn't get it.

Ever the peacekeeper, Kelsey had warned her on the phone before she got here not to ask about the seven-year separation, though. And that was easy for her to say. Kelsey could afford to speak casually about their long time with no contact from the guys.

She had Tavish back.

Until Kelsey's call a few days ago, Amber had been almost sure Tomas was long dead. She had tried contacting his parents, but they hadn't returned any of her calls, texts, emails, or letters. She had shown up as usual at their Renaissance Fairee the first two summers, but they had found a way to completely ignore her, and none of the faire people would talk about any of their gang of friends.

The whole thing was weird as a goth guy at a shopping mall.

But she wouldn't get answers by moping. And anyway, soon Tomas would be here. She would finally be able to just ask him about it—and have fun cajoling the true answer out of that cryptic rascal—so Amber smiled at Tavish as nicely as she could, under the circumstances.

"Well I hope it's true. I hope he does come see you."

But they saw right through her. At least they were nice about it.

Tavish smiled back at her and winked.

"Yeah, I'll bet you're happy he's coming to see

me." He laughed a little.

Kelsey pushed her lips together in an attempt not to laugh at Amber — which saved her from being kicked under the table with one of Amber's heavy Doc Martin boots, unlike Tavish.

He took it like a man, though. Didn't even grunt.

Amber wrinkled her nose at him in congratulations, and he wrinkled his back.

"Well," said Kelsey, "it turns out not everyone was separated these past seven years. Jaelle and John stayed together."

Amber's jaw dropped.

"No way."

Kelsey unwrapped her flatware from the napkin and put it in her lap.

"Yep, they did, but we heard from him six months ago that they broke up."

The waitress came then with their food, and as she placed it in front of them and they all nodded at her politely, Amber thought about the wonderful summers they had all spent together in their teens at the Renaissance Fairee that Tavish and Tomas's parents ran with the help of Mike, Gabe, Jeff, and John's parents.

Back then, she'd been sure the guys had the coolest parents she'd ever meet. Not only had Dall & Emily and Peadar & Vange taught everyone in the Scottish guild Gaelic, but also they had let their sons' girlfriends use costumes from the costume shed instead of having to make their own when they first joined the guild — and had to change out of the English costumes they'd made when they joined the faire.

And she had spent four glorious fun-filled summers with her best boyfriend ever.

Tomas had Skyped with her every night during the school years, when they couldn't be together, and each new summer they had picked up right where they left off.

Until the day after he and Tavish turned eighteen. He hadn't been there since, and no one would talk about him. Until now. Tavish and Kelsey were saying precious little, but she got the impression that badgering them for info would make them shut down, maybe even send her away.

She raised her mug of ale in a toast.

"To reunions."

Her friends raised their mugs.

"To reunions."

After they drank up, it was Amber's turn to change the subject. She asked Kelsey logistical questions about the dig, and the two of them amicably discussed artifact cataloging methods through the rest of the meal and on the drive out to the dig.

As they talked, Amber finally understood why she had been invited to come here. She was going to be Kelsey's go-to person for practical hands-on advice.

Kelsey had a doctorate in Celtic Art History and her friend Sasha had a doctorate in Celtic Archaeology, but this was both of their first time in charge of a dig. Meanwhile, Amber had dropped out of beauty school six years ago to do grunt work on a dig — and never looked back. Her parents had known someone who got her involved in it, and she loved it.

Kelsey had lucked upon discovering a huge underground palace beneath Dunskey Castle here in Scotland. She had just been on the international news announcing her discovery, so now this was a world-famous dig that would be open to tourists and last ten years or more — and pay well.

Amber tried to sound businesslike and not show how giddy she felt.

"Yeah, Reichmann's method that we used in Mexico was my favorite. If you want, I'll help you organize it."

Kelsey turned her head toward the backseat and opened her eyes as big as she could and showed her teeth in a 'cat that ate the canary' kind of way.

"Oh that's just the beginning of what I brought you out here to help me with."

While she visited with her friend, Amber watched the city turn into green and gray mountains with deep green valleys between, punctuated by the occasional thistle bush or flock of sheep. Finally, they turned off the highway and drove out toward the sea, then parked amid twenty other cars in a field.

Kelsey looped her arm through Amber's, and the two of them marveled at the scene together as they walked from the car over toward a city of site trailers. Tavish carried all of her bags.

Well, Amber marveled while Kelsey kept

agreeing with her.

"Everything's as clean as it is in a nineteen fifties sitcom."

"I know. Isn't it amazing?"

"And even though it's all cloudy and overcast, I still wanna be outside here."

"Me too."

"And we're right next to the ocean."

"Yep, and Mr. Blair has promised us a motorboat so we can go to Ireland sometimes. I mean, even now we could just go to Portpatrick and hire someone to take us, but it's not the same."

"Wow. It couldn't get any better than this, could it. Thanks for bringing me in on this, Kel."

Kelsey reached over the front seat and squeezed her hand.

"I know that was a rhetorical question, but you haven't heard yet what some think is the best part."

Amber chuckled, looking at Tavish behind his back.

"Guys in kilts bring all the women breakfast in bed?"

Kelsey laughed and held up her phone.

"No! The underground castle is well ventilated by a series of small side caves, and near some of their openings, we can get cell reception."

Amber laughed.

"I'm not going to fall for that trick. You'll have to haze your new employee some other way."

Kelsey raised her eyebrows in a 'you'll see' kind of expression and stopped in front of a two-bedroom trailer.

"This one's mine and Sasha's, but she's away for a while."

They put Amber's things in one of the bedrooms, where she chased Tavish out and hurriedly changed into black jeans and a black hoodie, then turned to Kelsey.

"Well, this is a nice trailer and all, but let's get out to the dig site."

Kelsey laughed.

Soon, they were rushing over toward the ruins of a tower house that stood just in front of a drop-off that led down to the ocean. It was overcast and misty, but as Amber looked out into the fog, she could imagine seeing Ireland in the distance. It made her smile, having something to look forward to amid the wonder of already being here and the prospect of seeing Tomas again soon.

When they got close to the tower house, Amber saw that the drop down to the sea was quite a long one.

"So the dig is inside these cliffs?"

Tavish nodded, leading her over to an open cellar door.

"Aye, and you get down to it through this hatch."

Amber made sure he noticed when she rolled her eyes at him for saying Aye instead of yes.

When they got closer to the hatch, she could see that a ladder had been installed.

"How do you suppose they got down here before the ladder? Jumped down in long skirts and kilts? Doesn't seem very practical."

Tavish pointed over to an area east of the tower house.

"Oh, this is a newer entrance. In the old time, they go... went in down the stairs over there. We don't use them, because we're trying to preserve them."

Amber pursed her lips together and tittered her head back-and-forth, imitating his serious tone and how important he looked and sounded, and then she commented to Kelsey.

"I thought you were the one who'd studied all this stuff. Why is he the one sounding like a professor of ancient Celtic architecture?"

Kelsey and Tavish shared a look, and then Kelsey burst out laughing.

"I was asking myself the same thing when I first got here, believe me. But Tavish has been around here a lot, so on this particular site, he's at least as much of an expert as I am."

Tavish went down the ladder and stood at the bottom, holding up his hand to steady Amber in case she needed it, for which she was grateful. But not wishing to tell him so — and swell his head up bigger than it already was — she continued to tease him about how much he knew about the dig.

"Well you can't have been here that much longer than Kelsey. I mean, didn't you say Mr. Blair just took ownership of this property three months ago?"

But then she got down inside the root cellar and was watching Kelsey open a secret door using a series of ancient bricks with Celtic markings all over them, and she forgot all about teasing Tavish. If that wasn't enough, the door opened into a secret passageway full of these Celtic runes, which led to a three-way intersection full of even more of them, and then she was in a secret room with the age-old drawings all over it.

Right out of her head flew all thoughts about how long Tavish had been at the site or even how much he knew. She just stood there with her jaw hanging open and her eyes wide while Kelsey and Tavish turned on the lights they had rigged down here.

Kelsey came and stood beside her.

"I thought I'd have you start in here, dusting off these runes so we can seal them against future damage."

Refusing to take her eyes off all the ancient stone-carved symbols, Amber did the best she could to nod her head yes.

~*~

The next day, Amber could barely contain her excitement as she watched the car drive up the road toward the dig site. She hadn't seen Tomas in seven years. She was intensely curious to see how he had changed and to hear what he'd been up to. She hoped he wasn't fat. Yuck. Did he have a fun job like hers? Or did he work in an office somewhere? She really hoped the latter wasn't the case.

She was rocking forward and back from her toes to her heels by the time the car pulled up, and she had to consciously make herself stop so as not to look silly.

The car had tinted windows, so her curiosity was still unsatisfied.

Should she rush up to the car and be the one to greet him when he stepped out? Her hesitation gave the opportunity to Tavish instead. That was probably better. Tavish had been the one to invite him after all. And they were brothers. Twins. Non-identical twins, but still...

And then the car door opened.

Yum.

Tomas was still tall and lean. He had shaggy hair and wore a flowy poet's shirt. He had a tiny hint of a mustache and no beard, thank God.

The two brothers embraced, and Amber found herself smiling wistfully at them. How nice. She was glad her own brothers and sister had never lost touch with her.

Okay, Tavish and Tomas had turned around, and Tomas was looking over the site. Now was a good time for her to go say hi.

As she rushed over there, she pulled up the long sleeves of her flowing black blouse, just in case he wanted to shake hands instead of giving her a hug. You can presume too much after seven years, after all. Even in her heavy boots, she was jogging by the time she got to him.

Oddly, he still hadn't met her eyes. When she was right in front of him, though, he didn't have a choice.

A handshake it was, then. She held out her hand to him.

"Welcome to Scotland, Tomas."

She made her smile as warm and welcoming as she could. Maybe he would stay a while and they'd get a chance to rekindle—

The most grating female voice Amber had ever heard came to her ears across the top of the car in a lilting Southern accent.

"Tomas honey, come over here and help me with this door, please."

The tone was sweet and should've been pleasing, but something about that voice just hurt her ears.

Probably the 'honey' part.

Dread sank into Amber as she looked over at the woman who was obviously Tomas's girlfriend. While Amber was dark-haired and olive skinned, this woman was honey blonde with alabaster skin. While Amber was quirky and artsy and thought of herself as fun-loving, this woman was stately and imperious. There was no way she could compete with such a woman. The two of them had absolutely nothing in common except their interest in Tomas. You could tell just by looking.

Kelsey had run up beside her. She grabbed ahold of her arm, apparently for support. Then Kelsey gasped, let go of Amber's arm, and grabbed Tavish's.

"That's Sulis!" Kelsey hissed.

Tavish's forehead wrinkled.

"Are you sure?"

"Yes!"

Amber put her hand on Kelsey's shoulder.

"What's the matter? Who's Sulis?"

Tavish rubbed his eyes and put his hand over his mouth, leaning down on it.

Kelsey swallowed, still staring at Tomas and his girlfriend over the top of their rental car.

"Sulis is friends with the druids who control Tavish."

"What?"

JANE STAIN

Dhà (2)

What Kelsey said had minorly alarmed Amber and piqued a little curiosity, but mostly she just wanted to crawl under a rock and hide. She'd left a perfectly good job at the dig in Mexico and come all the way to Scotland — pretty much just to be with Tomas. On hearing that Tavish was here, she'd just assumed Tomas would be here too, single and ready to pick up where they had left off. It had never occurred to her he might have a girlfriend. She was so stupid. She should've asked ahead of time. Should've asked Tavish for Tomas's number and called Tomas herself and asked if he was single.

Now she wished she had rented her own car and driven herself here, so she could just leave right now. But she hadn't. Fiddling with her phone in her pocket, she debated calling a cab. But it would be so expensive to take a cab to the airport. Which wouldn't be a problem if she hadn't just quit her job. Ugh! And since every dig had a waiting list of workers ten pages long, she knew her job was long gone by now.

While she debated this silently in her mind, her body moved past people of its own accord, getting them out of her line of sight so she could follow Tomas's movements. It was stupid, but she couldn't help it. Her brain knew she should go back to Kelsey's trailer and wait there until Kelsey came so she could get a ride back to the airport. But her heart kept her body right here. Watching him. If she was honest, she'd admit to herself that she was pining after him. How pathetic.

He went over to help Sulis get out of the car, then back toward the trunk.

But Sulis tossed her hand in the air cavalierly and gestured over toward Tavish as if she were the most gracious being in the world — and spoke in her sickly sweet Southern drawl.

"Oh you can get that later. Right now you should really talk to your brother. We came all the way out here just to see him, after all."

He stopped and came back to her and stood there like a little boy next to his mom. Or a dog with its mistress.

She brought his arm out and looped hers through it like some Victorian lady. "Let's go on over and you can introduce me."

Pretty much everyone had stopped what they were doing to watch the show. Amber looked around, and she and Kelsey were the only women there besides Sulis.

Kelsey was looking at Amber with an apology and a lot of guilt in her eyes.

All of the men — Mr. Blair, Tavish, and all the rest of the construction workers — were looking at Sulis as if she were something good to eat.

Tomas and Sulis walked around their car arm in arm, and Sulis smiled at Tavish indulgently with her one hand on his brother's chest and her other arm looped through his brother's arm. And then instead of waiting for an introduction, she asserted her own.

"Well you must be Tavish. I've heard so much about you. You're just as handsome as I thought you would be." Completely ignoring Kelsey — who was obviously with Tavish, having her arm through his in much the same way as Sulis was holding onto his brother — Sulis just smiled at Tavish and batted her eyelashes. Well, she didn't quite bat her eyelashes, but she might as well have.

Tavish was tongue-tied, and under ordinary circumstances, Amber would've admired anyone who could accomplish that. But this was war.

Amber straightened her back and un-hunched her shoulders. War was not the time to slouch. Besides, Sulis's posture was perfect, and Amber didn't want to give the woman any more advantage than she clearly already had.

Kelsey knew it was war, too, because without

reaching out to the woman at all, in fact blatantly keeping her hands resting on Tavish, Kelsey asserted her own sarcastically sweet introduction.

"Well it's so nice to meet you, Sulis. We don't know much about you at all. Please, tell us the story of how you met Tomas — and don't forget to tell us how long ago that was." Kelsey gave the woman her own saccharin smile in perfect imitation of the other. "Please."

Admiring her friend's chutzpah, Amber winked at Kelsey.

Kelsey winked back.

But to Kelsey's obvious chagrin, Sulis took charge just by starting to walk. Like a tigress in high heels, swinging her imaginary tail back and forth with her elegant yet short skirt, she led everyone on a leisurely stroll toward the sea cliff, where the sun was just starting to set.

Even the construction workers walked with her, visibly enthralled with the way Sulis walked, the way she carried herself, how pretty she was, and whatever else men got enthralled about.

Kelsey was in charge of the dig, but Tavish was the construction foreman. Kelsey wisely didn't tell the men to get back to work, although Amber could tell she was dying to deprive Sulis of her audience.

As the statuesque blonde strolled past the other cars and the trailers toward the gorgeous view ahead — sort of dragging Tomas along with her by the arm, not that anyone but Amber and Kelsey noticed — she did tell the story of her and Tomas's meeting. However, she told it in a way that made her storytelling seem like it was her idea, rather than an answer to Kelsey's demand.

"Oh, it was so romantic. I was in the area with my... religious group. We'd had a... celebration that day, but there was nothing scheduled for that evening. So I ducked into the cutest antique shop I ever did see — you know, just to pass the time."

She smiled at all the men around her, and they nodded and smiled back at her encouragingly, eating up every word she said.

If it weren't for Kelsey's being here, Amber would've gone back to her trailer rather than hear this drivel. She met Kelsey's eye behind Sulis's back and put her finger down her throat and pretended like she was making herself vomit.

Kelsey mustered a tiny smile in response.

Now approaching the wonderful view down the cliffs of the sea crashing on the rocks below — and Ireland peeking out of the multicolored mist in the distance — Sulis gestured proudly as if this were all her creation, enjoyed the appreciative nods from the men, and then continued her story.

"Well, of course Tomas was the only one working in the antique store. His parents run it, you know — I mean, they own it." She cuddled up next to him with her cheek next to his cheek in a way that made Amber want to vomit for real. "And Tomas will own it after they're gone. Won't you, dear."

Amber gave Kelsey a "yeah right" look. Tomas and Tavish had two more brothers and a sister, and Sulis obviously didn't know that — but she was stupid not to include Tavish in her flattery about owning the antique store.

Kelsey gave Amber a worried look in return. Uh oh.

But Tavish didn't say anything, and Tomas just nodded at Sulis with a big dopey grin on his face.

And Amber's heart dropped into her stomach as Sulis reached up over her shoulder and slowly ran her fingers along Tomas's jaw, making him close his eyes in apparent ecstasy while she continued her tale.

"So, you know how it is, gentlemen. I looked at all the wonderful antiques in his parents' store, asking him to show me how this dagger works and how that sword hefts. Meanwhile, between demonstrations of his fighting prowess, he kept looking at me. Eventually he asked me out, and the rest is history."

Kelsey shrugged and put her hand out as if to say "And?" But when that didn't produce any results, she put her hands on her hips in frustration and voiced the question that was on Amber's mind too, because it didn't make sense.

"Hold on a minute. You said you were just in the area for a religious gathering. If you weren't from around there, then how did you and Tomas keep seeing each other?"

Sulis gave Tomas a very pretty smile and straightened the collar on his poet's shirt, which didn't need straightening at all.

"Well, Tomas didn't want to be without me after even that first meeting."

She looked around at all the men and received the confirmation she obviously wanted: from the look of their smiles and nods, none of them wanted to be without her after this first meeting, either.

"So, he moved to Greenwich Village with me after my week's vacation was over."

She dramatically sighed as if she'd just remembered something.

"Oh, and to answer your other question, Kelsey..."

She smiled prettily at Kelsey, but obviously it was for the benefit of the men, because Kelsey was scowling at her. So was Amber, but Sulis was plainly just ignoring her.

"That was almost exactly two months ago, when Tomas moved with me to Greenwich Village. So as you can imagine, we've been really busy."

She tilted her head just so then, and all the men grinned. Some of them actually giggled. She cupped Tavish's face with her hand.

"Otherwise, Tavish, I'm sure he would've come to see you sooner."

Surprisingly, at this, Tomas woke up from his zombielike state and said more than 'Yes, Sulis; right away, Sulis; let me be your slave, Sulis.'

"Oh, I don't know about that. My brother's been off gallivanting around on his own ever since we turned twenty five. He doesn't need me anymore."

At that, Sulis turned to him with a hard look in her eye. It was the kind of look that would make

27

most men break up with a woman right there and then — cold and calculating and obviously uncaring. And then she whispered something unintelligible in his ear before she put on a sweet face again and spoke up for her audience.

"Tomas honey, I'm more tired from our trip over here to Scotland than I at first thought. I'm sure these people put on a lovely spread, but I want to go eat dinner near the hotel. Be a love and go get the car, will you?"

Amber could barely control her excitement, waiting for him to explode at Sulis for ordering him around, let alone looking at him with such contempt. This was going to be good.

To her shock, he calmly nodded and started walking toward their rental car as if she'd never looked at him like he was a slave that she could whip for disobeying her. Nuh uh. This was so not the Tomas she knew and loved. No. Something was wrong with him. He must be on cold meds or something, and if so, he shouldn't be driving!

Amber went to follow him.

But she felt an arm around her waist, jerking her to a stop.

Amber turned to tell Kelsey it was fine, that she was just going to make sure Tomas was okay to drive. That she knew what she was doing.

But it was Sulis.

"Hello, doll face. I don't believe I've had the pleasure of making your acquaintance. I'm Tomas's girlfriend, and I'd really appreciate it if you didn't go with him to the car."

Amber saw red and twisted out of the

woman's grasp. Who was she to say where Amber should go? This witch with a B might be his girlfriend, but...

"Listen, Sulis. I've known Tomas for eleven years. You may be his girlfriend right now, but I am his friend-friend. If I want to talk to him, then I am going to talk to him, and you can complain all you want, but you aren't going to stop me, so just get out of my way before I—"

Of all people, Tavish came over with a take-charge attitude and put his hands between Amber and the other woman. And addressed himself to Amber.

"Now Amber, Sulis has a point. She is Tomas's current girlfriend, so I think you ought to do as she asks."

What!

Amber looked over at Kelsey and gave her a look — asking for verification that Tavish was being nuts.

Kelsey blinked a few times to show that she agreed, but then she put on a reasonable face and walked over and took Amber's hand.

"Amber, I think you and I ought to go back to my trailer and rest a bit."

Tomas drove up then and parked between Amber and Sulis, who made a pretty show of waving goodbye to Amber over the top of the car. While the look in her eyes said 'Sulis one, Amber zero,' she called out in her cloying Southern accent.

"I think that's a good idea Kelsey. You get that girl to rest up a bit and listen to Tomas's brother, who's trying to talk some sense into her." She turned and smiled and waved at all the men gathered around. "We'll see y'all tomorrow. Bye now."

All the men smiled at her and waved.

"Bye."

~*~

Once she and Kelsey were in their trailer and had privacy, Amber blurted out what was on her mind.

"I can't believe I came all the way out here thinking I was gonna see Tomas and not realizing he might have a girlfriend. I'm so stupid, Kelsey. Why am I out there even arguing with her when she obviously has a claim on him? He looks at her with such puppy dog eyes, I can't even stand to be around them. Maybe they won't be here very long and I can come back after they're gone, but for now, I've got to leave. I was thinking I'd fly back home, but really I can just go stay in a hotel far enough away from here that I won't see them. If you just take me into town, I can rent a car and handle everything on my own. I'm sorry to do this to you, but —"

But Kelsey was shaking her head no and had a panicked look on her face and kept trying to interrupt. Finally, Amber stopped and let Kelsey talk.

"Amber, Sulis is a druid, and she's using her magic to compel Tomas —"

What? Amber crossed her arms and raised an eyebrow at Kelsey.

"You've got to be kidding me. You know, you

always had a vivid imagination, and that was fun when we were teens. But we're grown women now. You've got a PhD, Kelsey. You don't have to make stuff up anymore to get attention—"

But Kelsey was shaking her head no and holding her palms out. And laughing just a tiny bit.

"I know it sounds like something I would have made up when we were younger, but think about it... if you remember the look in Tomas's eyes — the look in all the men's eyes — you'll know what I'm saying is the truth. Sulis has a way of bewitching men so that they see her as some sort of 'do no wrong' person."

Yeah. That was exactly what Amber had been thinking.

Despite how stupid it sounded, she found herself actually entertaining the idea that Sulis was using magic. Because really, the woman was nasty. And in Amber's experience, most men saw through that stuff. But not around this woman they didn't. There had to be a reason. Sulis was beautiful and charming, yes, but she was only human... or maybe she wasn't.

Amber gave her friend a speculative look.

"Okay, you're right about that. The men were falling all over each other trying to please her, all two dozen of them. I've never seen anything like it. I'm listening."

Kelsey nodded sharply.

"Darn straight I'm right about that. Her spell doesn't seem to work on women, but it sure is working on the men. She has them all wrapped

31

around her little finger." Kelsey met Amber's gaze and held it with an intense look of her own. "Please don't go. Tomas needs our help, and you may be the only one who can get through to him."

Amber lowered her chin and looked up at Kelsey, making her skull earrings jiggle painfully on her ears.

"Me? Why me? He hasn't said a word to me the whole time he's been here."

Kelsey gave her a look that said, 'The whole time he's been here? It's only been half an hour.' But when she actually spoke, her voice was sincere.

"Because you care about him so much. Tavish does too, but Tomas is angry at Tavish, so his brother may not be able to get through to him. You can't tell me you didn't notice?"

Trì (3)

That night, Amber lay awake in her tiny trailer bedroom, tossing and turning. Everything Sulis had said kept running through her mind, and over and over again she saw how dead Tomas's eyes looked, and how he followed Sulis around — not even like a little puppy. Puppies were alive. He was lifeless. More like a slave. It tore her up inside.

Finally, she gave in and got up. No, there was nothing she could do to help Tomas tonight, but she knew herself well. When something was on her mind, her body needed to get good and tired, or she would never fall asleep. And then she would be useless at helping him, not to mention useless at work tomorrow.

Normally, on days when her coworkers didn't organize a basketball game — the real kind, with fruit baskets hung in trees out there near the dig site in Mexico — she did jumping jacks and then jogged in place. But that would shake the 'check' out of this trailer and wake Kelsey up. There was no need for both of them to pass a sleepless night.

Besides, after eleven years of only dreaming about being here someday, she was finally in Scotland! And the full moon was shining through the window.

Not bothering with any makeup or jewelry, she quickly dressed in black sweats, her older pair of Doc Martin boots, and her coat, then snuck outside into the damp night air. Looking up at a bazillion stars despite the full moon, she popped in her ear buds and cranked up the music, then walk-jog-danced along the cliffs over the ocean.

It was a magical clear September night even if it was freezing cold here.

Shoving her hands into her pockets, she made a mental note to get some mittens next time someone went to town. And a thick wool scarf to put over her mouth and nose. She shuddered. Bbrrr! For now, she pulled up the hood of her sweatshirt and drew the drawstring tight, tying it in a bow, then stuffed her hands in her pockets.

But it really was beautiful here.

Moonlight hit the ripples in the ocean on her

left and the grey stone hills that surrounded the grassy valley on her right, yet she could still see more stars than she ever had at home — or on any other dig.

At the same time, it was rugged and untamed. But that added to Scotland's beauty.

Below the craggy cliffs, the waves sprayed up white moonlit foam when they crashed against the rocks, breaking into different intricate patterns every time that seemed to expand to the beat of her music.

"Cool," she said aloud before continuing to dance-jog along the pathway.

When it turned to the right and Port Patrick loomed down on her left, she felt tired enough to sleep. Regretting having come so far and needing to walk all that way back, she turned around.

She was as close to the edge of the cliff as she dared go, looking down to watch the waves crash against the rocks and bobbing her head to the beat of the music when out of nowhere, someone in a white hooded robe ran at her.

Her instinct was to shrink away from the running man, but her experience in basketball told her to run toward him instead. So that was what she did, knowing full well that if she hadn't been in such good shape, she would have been startled into falling off the cliff for sure.

It seemed to be the robed man's intent to make her fall off the cliff, because he kept on running toward her, not backing down and not turning aside.

She changed her course a bit so that she was

running more toward the trailers and less toward the man, surging with all she had to get out of this path and run back there before he would get to her.

But he was faster than her. Even running all out, she could tell he would get to her before she could get back to the dig camp.

So she changed tactics again.

Pivoting hard to her left, she ran away from the cliffs toward the grass, where at least he couldn't push her off the cliff. She was getting winded now, though. She wouldn't have much strength left to fight him once he caught up to her.

Fortunately, she was now within earshot of the trailers. If anyone happened to be outside.

She stopped suddenly, took in as deep a breath as she could, and screamed for all she was worth.

The man laughed just before he got to her. A harsh, cruel laugh.

And then he grunted and went down.

He must've tripped. She made herself start running again, to take advantage of this trick fate chose to play on him. But she was nearly spent. She'd been running all out for almost a mile. And besides, curiosity got the best of her.

She firmly planted her feet far enough apart that she couldn't be knocked over easily and then looked over her shoulder.

Tomas was here. He had tackled the man in white, and the two of them were wrestling on the ground.

Exhilaration swelled in her heart. Tomas had come to save her.

And at the very same time, a new fear bloomed in her head. Fear for his safety now, rather than hers.

She looked around for a rock or a stick, anything she could use to hit the robed man in the head, if given the chance.

But white-robe-man got up and ran off.

Suddenly exhausted now that she felt safe and was sure Tomas would be safe, Amber put her hands on her thighs and gulped in the air.

Tomas stood back there where he'd wrestled with her attacker, looking past her at the trailers. He had his arms crossed, but he wasn't angry. It was more like his arms were two doors that he was closing in front of himself.

In light of that, what he said really caught her off guard. It was so familiar and informal that it made her feel like there hadn't been a seven-year separation between them. Like this was just another day the two of them were hanging out together in a long string of such days.

The way things had been between them seven plus years ago.

"You look better without all that black stuff on your mouth."

Finally, she'd caught enough breath to speak. She said the first thing that came to her mind.

"What are you doing here so late? I thought you were staying at a hotel in town."

Tomas started walking quickly back toward the dig's trailer town.

"I'm just out for a walk."

She rolled her eyes out of habit, but he was looking ahead and didn't see. She had to jog to keep up with him.

"I know that, but why are you walking here? I thought you and ... that you went back to town, to your hotel."

He kept walking on in silence.

And again, she felt foolish. Yeah, he'd been nice enough to come and save her, but he was someone else's boyfriend now. He didn't have to tell her anything about why he was here, what he was doing out at night, or anything. She had to remember that.

It was hard, though.

Walking with him like this — at night on the grass with the stars above them in the bright moonlight — well, it reminded her of many such nights they used to spend when they were together. He'd been such a romantic, inviting her to take walks in the moonlight on the grass and then gazing deep into her eyes and baring his soul to her before each kiss...

Stop it.

Yes, Tomas needed her to get through to him and get him away from Sulis. That much Kelsey had convinced her of. But that didn't mean she and Tomas would be back together again. Look at him, she told herself. He's looking off at the boring trailers. He isn't the least bit interested in you. Yeah, he cares enough to save you from some white-robed weirdo, but he would do that for anyone.

She wasn't special to him. Not anymore.

But then when they entered the dig camp, he turned to look at her finally. And rather than the studied indifference and patience — or even just the friend-zoning she had been expecting — the look on his face was ... uncertain. Puzzled, even. Like he had just woken up in a strange place and wasn't sure how he'd gotten there.

"Sulis said she wanted to walk on the grass in the moonlight, but that I couldn't come with her. I insisted on driving her here, and then I just hung out in the car — until I saw you go walking off toward the cliffs."

She raised her eyebrows at him and gave him a goofy grin.

"So if I hadn't taken a walk out toward the cliffs, you'd still be just sitting in the car all alone? Were you at least reading a book or something? Listening to your music? Do you still like Celtic rock?"

He pursed his lips and moved his eyes from side to side as if he could find the answer to her question in their surroundings. Finally, he shook his head no and gave her a sheepish grin.

"Yeah, I still like Celtic rock, but no, no I wasn't listening to music or reading or anything. Just sitting there." He rumpled his eyebrows a little bit. "Are you saying I should thank you for relieving my boredom?"

Maybe Kelsey was right. Just her being with him seemed to be working. His personality was peeking out behind the dull lifeless eyes — and maybe it was her imagination, but they seemed to be getting a little twinkly, a little less absent.

Amber laughed just a little, just enough to hopefully lighten this mood that was too somber even for a Goth girl.

"Uh huh."

He gave her a small amused smile.

"Okay. Thanks."

She gave him one back.

"You're welcome. Oh, and by the way, thanks for stopping that guy from running me off the cliff."

He nodded his head sideways once.

"You're welcome."

Amber's analytical brain was pointing out that since the mood was now light and they were joking around, it would be a good time to ask him what was going on.

And before her heart could talk her out of it — before her love for him and yearning for him could convince her to just enjoy his company for however long he wanted to share it with her, to live in the moment and cherish it for what it was — she blurted out the questions that were on her mind.

"Tomas, who was that guy? Why was he wearing a white robe? What is Sulis doing walking around in the moonlight, and why can't you go with her?"

They had reached Kelsey's trailer. Just as her heart had feared, her questions made him back away from her, from the familiarity they were beginning to enjoy again with each other. He looked out to the grassy fields where Sulis must be walking.

He said just one more thing over his shoulder as he walked away toward his rental car.

"No more walks after dark, Amber."

Amber just stood there. She watched him get in his car and close the door, but then when he just sat there waiting for some other woman and didn't look at her, she felt alone again.

Thanking the stars above that she was so tired, she snuck back into bed and fell fast asleep.

~*~

She dreamed that she and Kelsey were in the underground castle together, the site of the dig. Only now it was new inside. All the chiseled stone pictures of snakes, dogs, birds, human anatomy, flowers, and other natural things on the walls, ceiling, and floor practically gleamed with newness. And there was furniture in the rooms. It was odd furniture, made of carved wood but in shapes she'd never seen before. There were odd niches in every room whose purpose Amber couldn't even guess at they were so foreign, and the beds were carved out of the native stone of the place in shapes like giant bowls, and full of pillows shaped like apples and pears and grapes.

Standing still yet flying up and down and sideways together as if they were on a magic painter's lift, she and Kelsey went on a whirlwind tour of the underground Celtic palace, seeing dozens of rooms in only a minute.

They stopped inside a large room with a huge golden throne. It looked heavy. How would they ever get it out without destroying the place? She looked all around for a way to get such a large object out, but saw none. How had it gotten in here? Had the ancient Celts made it down here, thousands of years ago?

Amber was imagining she saw long lines of Celtic men and women with patterns tattooed on their faces and all over their bodies bringing endless pieces of gold down here for the head druid to melt in an iron pot over a roaring fire when Kelsey spoke.

"I'm here with you for real, Amber. This is more than just a dream. No one can hear what we say when I visit you in your dreams. It's the safest way to make plans and compare notes."

What the...? To give herself time to think and analyze the situation, Amber crossed her arms and blinked a few times.

"Okay, this is weird. But what's the harm in talking to you in my dream, right? I'm ninety nine point nine, nine, nine percent sure that tomorrow you'll have no idea what's been said in this dream. But weird things are going on. So just to test it, tomorrow I'll casually say something innocuous that we've said in this dream. If this is real and you remember what we said, then wink at me. If this is just a dream, then of course you won't wink at me, and I'll know."

Kelsey pursed her lips and nodded at Amber.

"Good plan. Okay, so here's what I think we should do about Sulis —"

Amber put a hand on her friend's shoulder and

shook her head no — in fact, she shook her friend's whole body, trying to get her attention.

"Oh, we've got much bigger problems than Sulis."

Kelsey lowered her chin and raised her eyebrows.

"Bigger than Sulis?"

Amber took a big breath and let it out.

"Oh yeah. Bigger than a whole pack of Sulises walking on a shoe store's worth of high heels."

She told her friend what had just happened to her, with the white robed guy chasing after her and Tomas saving her.

Kelsey's face went white.

"Are you sure he was wearing a white robe?"

What did she mean, was she sure?

"Uh, yeah. But what's the big deal about a white robe? I was kind of more alarmed with the fact that he was trying to make me Fall. Off. The. Cliff."

Kelsey put her arm around Amber and hugged her.

"Of course that part's more disturbing. Sorry. It's just that while Sasha and I were at Celtic University, we studied druids, who were Celtic priests. They wore white linen robes during their ceremonies, which were always out in nature..." Kelsey gasped. "And it was a full moon last night."

Amber raised her eyebrows.

Kelsey took a deep breath and spoke fast.

"Druids were nature worshipers. They held their ceremonies in sacred groves of trees —

which they fortified with standing stones once the Romans started coming after them. And the movements of the moon and the planets have to do with it also…"

Amber laughed and playfully nudged Kelsey's arm with the back of her hand.

"You said 'have to do with it' instead of 'had to do with it.'"

But her friend didn't laugh.

Amber tapped her with the back of her hand again.

"Come on, that's funny."

Kelsey turned around until she was staring Amber in the face, inches away from her, very intense.

"Tomas said Sulis wanted to walk on the green grass in the moonlight last night, right?"

Ceithir (4)

The next morning, Amber showered, did her long dark hair in a more romantic style, removed her black nail polish, and did her makeup normal instead of Goth. Just for variety. What Tomas said had nothing to do with it. She just had more personality than to always wear the same look, was all. She checked herself twice in the mirror, adjusting first her hair and then the lay of her clothes before she was satisfied.

When Amber came out of her bedroom dressed for work in her Doc Martin boots, jeans, and a white blouse so long it might as well have been a dress, Kelsey was busy scrambling eggs.

Amber went into the refrigerator and got out the orange juice.

"It was a full moon last night."

Kelsey paused for a moment at stirring her scrambled eggs, and when their eyes met while Amber was on her way into the cupboard to get the juice glasses — Kelsey winked at her.

A rush of adrenaline went through Amber, and she almost dropped the glasses. She managed to put them down on the counter, but her hand shook so much when she tried to pour that she gave up and set the carton down.

Kelsey handed her the spatula.

"Here, you stir the eggs. I'll pour the juice."

When they both had their food and sat facing each other, Amber opened her mouth to say something.

But Kelsey shook her head no and took a sip of her juice, staring at Amber significantly over the top of the glass.

"I hope you have sweet dreams tonight."

Oh.

They could only talk in their dreams.

Because people might be listening.

Amber nodded, and they finished their breakfast and went down inside the underground castle. Amber saw it with new eyes after that tour in her dream the night before, recognizing the odd niches in each room and seeing the barest hints of decoration behind all the layers of dust and cobwebs. Excited again about working here, she grabbed Kelsey by the arm and gestured to include the whole underground area.

"I might not have the book learning you do, but my experience tells me how this is supposed to work. You haven't gotten very far down in your dig, so you can't have turned up much of anything to base theories of origin on. How do you know what it looked like down here when it was new?"

Kelsey smiled at a construction worker passing by before turning to Amber with wide eyes.

"Are you kidding? Only in my wildest dreams would I know that!"

Slowly nodding yes, Amber let go of her friend's arm. Okay, the weird magic stuff was way more secret than she thought.

The two of them talked business for an hour — with Kelsey asking a million questions about where to keep the cataloging stuff and how to organize everything — and then Amber got her tools off a table that stood in the center of a long hallway and moved toward the room she was working on, speaking to Kelsey over her shoulder.

"I can see we need to talk a lot more about your dreams. See you at lunch?"

Kelsey nodded matter-of-factly and waved as she walked down the hall.

Amber spent the next hour brushing dust and cobwebs out of a huge tree carved in the floor of the secret room she was working on, but all the while her mind was scheming. Tomas knew more than he let on about all this weird magic stuff. And he knew who the white robe guy was, she could tell by the way he looked at the man.

How should she go about getting Tomas alone so she could ask him about the man? She would have to get Sulis busy doing something else. Her favorite idea there was spilling something all over blondie's designer clothes, but then she would probably just demand that Tomas drive her back to their hotel...

Before she could act on any of her ideas, however, Tomas came into her workroom.

His vacant zombielike eyes looked away from hers almost as soon as he came in, and then he turned to study the part of the tree she was done brushing free of debris and spoke offhandedly, in a barely audible voice.

"Why did you come here to Scotland?"

She sighed. She couldn't exactly tell him the truth, which would be 'I came to see you, of course. I thought we could pick right up where we left off in our relationship before you disappeared on me the day after your eighteenth birthday. I figured since Kelsey and Tavish were back together, it only made sense that you and I would be back together. Thought all I'd have to do was show up, and you'd welcome me back into your arms.'

No, she couldn't give out any hint she wanted to talk about that, or he would be stricken with the fear of his creepy girlfriend and bolt out the door. Amber knew that in her gut. And because her heart ached so for him, she knew her ache for him would show in her eyes, here under the bright work lights. So she didn't even dare look at him, but made a point of keeping her eyes on the carved-out tree as well, while she formulated her answer.

She did come up with something truthful she could tell him.

"Kelsey called and begged me to come help her. She just got her doctorate in Celtic Art History, you know, but she doesn't have much experience at dig sites. Well, I've spent the last six years working at them, so I'm helping her in lots of little ways only a real friend can."

She kept working while he slowly wandered around the large room, aimlessly looking at the wall carvings that were still barely legible beneath all the dirt and grime. When he was back near the doorway a quarter hour later, he spoke again.

He kept asking her pretty much the same thing: why was she here. Each time he asked, he would be near the door, looking like he was going to leave as soon as she answered.

Leave and go report back to Sulis.

For all Amber knew, Sulis had sent Tomas in here to ask her that very question. The thought enraged her, made her want to get up and go find that woman and tell her to mind her own business — and to admit that Tomas had friends and family who deserved to spend time with him.

But all of Amber's instincts told her to keep Tomas here in this room with her as long as she could.

So each time he asked why she'd come here, she scrambled her brains for a more interesting way to answer. Her aim was to keep adding more layers of meaning and connection and common history to her answer, yet to always be truthful. And she always emphasized that she was Kelsey's true friend — and by extension, she hoped she was reminding Tomas that she was his true friend.

She cared about him, and this was the hardest thing she'd ever done: telling him she cared about him without appearing to be doing so. Because again, her gut told her that the slightest appearance of her reaching out to him would trigger some sort of fear his faker of a girlfriend had implanted in him. Because Kelsey was clearly right: this was not the real Tomas. That woman had used magic or hypnosis or threats or something in order to charm him into submission to her.

And Amber had to keep telling herself his distance was a product of whatever spell Sulis had put on him, that it wasn't his decision to be like that. But his coldness hurt nonetheless.

By the fourth time he asked, he had been there in the secret room alone with Amber an hour — and she was blinking back tears when she answered his 'why are you here' question.

"A bunch of memories came back to me when Kelsey called, and I couldn't wait to see her and Tavish and you and everybody else again."

He wandered around some more. Was it her imagination, or was he staying closer and closer to her the longer he was here?

He asked it again, but this time he was definitely closer to her. And looking her in the eye. And rather than cold and distant, he looked … lost. Confused. His voice sounded that way, too.

"Why are you here?"

She longed to stand up and give him a hug, to remind him who she was and how much she had missed him. To ask why he had disappeared from her life. To tell him she still loved him and ask didn't he love her? But what did she dare do but answer his question?

Well, she could drag as much connection to him into her answer as possible, that was what.

"I've had a great time working at digs in Mexico and South America these past six years, but remember how all of us wanted to come to Scotland together — you & me, Tavish & Kelsey, John & Jaelle, Jeff & Ashley, Gabe & Lauren, and Mike & Sarah — how we would plan it out together, dreaming of some day when we'd all be here?"

He froze there, after she said that. It happened so abruptly that it broke her resolve not to look at him. There he was, still healthy and hale and handsome as ever, but shut down inside. It was as if someone had put opaque contact lenses on his eyes. He just wasn't all there.

But right this second, something different was happening. He had stopped and he was looking at her, right into her eyes. And she was looking into his, desperate to see him recognize her the way he had last night. She imagined she could see the wheels turning behind his eyes.

She imagined she was watching his very psyche battling the spell that held it captive.

After a long time as thinking goes — a minute or more — he nodded his head.

And now that she had drawn Tomas out a bit in the direction she truly wanted to, she didn't dare ask him about the white robed guy last night — whether he was a druid or not, and especially whether Sulis was a druid or not.

No. That would trigger some defensive part of the spell and undo all she had done over the last hour. She just knew it would. She had to keep things light, easy, unchallenging — or he would leave. She could get through to him if he would only stay awhile. She knew it. Just knew it.

There was one question she felt she could ask.

"What have you been doing with yourself these past seven years? Anything new?"

He paused, and the look on his face was heartbreaking. He looked like he couldn't remember the past seven years. But he kept quiet for a few moments, just looking into her eyes. Ever so gradually, his own eyes grew softer with recognition after a while.

When he spoke, his voice sounded almost normal. It reached deep inside of her and drew her to him, made her want to hug him and hold him close and love this blockage out of him.

But she knew she couldn't. Or else.

And it was so hard to see him like this. His face was not as animated as it normally was. Not nearly. He looked her in the eye though. That counted for a lot and relieved some of her hurt feelings.

"I've been taking some business classes," he said, "now that Mom and Dad and Vange and Peadar are talking about leaving me, Mike, Gabe, and Jeff in charge of the fair. They want to get Tavish and John more involved in the antique business."

She smiled at this.

Ha! So Sulis didn't know what she was talking about when it came to the antique store after all. It would be Tavish and John, not Tomas, who inherited the antiques business. Amber stopped working on the runes and settled back, leaning against the wall and really looking at Tomas.

"You get to be in charge of the fair? That's so cool."

He smiled. Actually smiled. It reached his eyes and everything.

She kept her smile up, careful to keep it friendly, though that was tough when his sudden joyous smile made her body want to tackle him like she would have seven years ago and...

She made herself focus on drawing his personality out, as if he were a stranger she was just getting to know.

"Have you and Mike and Gabe and Jeff worked out who will be in charge of what?"

He smiled again and nodded yes.

"I'm the only one taking business classes, so I'll be in charge of the money."

They laughed together, and it was the most wonderful feeling Amber'd had in years.

But never mind what her body wanted. That

was tough enough, but her own psyche was begging her to reach out to him and hug him and tell him how much she'd missed him — and to demand that he tell her why he had left her — why he'd disappeared from her life seven years ago.

Seeing how vulnerable he was, how hard he had to struggle just to remember his own life these past seven years, she told her psyche to shut up. This had to be about him. First. She promised the little abandoned girl inside of her that they two of them would get their turn. That once Tomas was himself again, she would insist on getting the answers they needed.

When he finished his brief laugh, Tomas continued talking.

"It's more complicated than that, of course. I'll be the business guy, which will include marketing the fair as well as the accounting and making sure vendors are licensed..."

She nodded.

"That's a lot of responsibility."

He let out a sigh.

"I know. It's much more responsibility than running an antique store." He looked at her with an 'oh yeah' look on his face, and then gestured toward her inclusively. "Well you know."

She smiled a goofy smile at him and nodded yes. Good. He remembered at least that she'd worked at the fair with him. Did he remember the rest? She was dying to ask him, but he still wasn't himself. Not by half.

"Yep, I know."

He relaxed a little and smiled, and she could have sworn he kicked some imaginary dust on the floor.

"Yeah, that's right, you did the fair with me for four years, so you know there's thousands of people involved who work there and hundreds of thousands of people all over the world who look forward to attending the fair every year..."

To draw his attention away from his embarrassment at forgetting she'd been there, she stood up. It worked. He watched her.

She smiled at him kindly.

"Yeah, that's a lot of responsibility you'll have. What are Mike, Gabe, and Jeff going to do?"

He chuckled at her joke about him doing everything.

"Well, seriously, there's still scheduling all the shows, and outreach to all the participants, getting the insurance — well I guess that's a business thing, so it's mine, too..."

She chuckled at his joke and then used one of the gestures they had used at the fair in their shows together, hoping the familiarity would draw him out more.

"Back up a minute. Did you say there were people all over the world looking forward to attending the fair every year?"

He had stayed by her side without wandering away for a good ten minutes now. This was working. Hope blossomed in her heart. And her body told her to grab him and kiss him and make him hers again. But her mind warned her that would be disastrous.

He stayed with her and nodded.

"Yeah."

She gently shook her head no, smiling at him incredulously.

"I didn't know that. I thought your fair was just in our town."

He scratched his head.

"Well, no. We have three different locations in the US while it's warm up there, and then when it's winter there, it's summer in Australia, so we have three locations down under, too." He wrinkled his nose up and twinkled his eyes at her. "Okay, I guess two countries isn't really all over the world."

She opened her mouth as wide as she could and let her jaw hang, bending her head forward a bit to show how shocked she was.

"And so you're going to be managing this whole thing? I guess you'll have business licenses to renew in six different locations — not to mention all the different taxes you'll have to file..."

He pushed his lips together and raised one eyebrow while nodding just a little in acknowledgment of a good summation of the scope of his duties.

"Mmhmm. But we have a good accountant and a good manager who will help train me before they retire — oh, you know them. Remember Edgar? Not Edgar the pickle monger, but Rowena's cousin Edgar?"

Her heart pounded in her chest with renewed hope. He was remembering!

She smiled and whirled her eyes around.

"Oh my gosh, don't tell me he's an accountant now? He could barely sit down, he was so hyper. But it was good for the show when he walked on stilts all the time!"

They laughed together.

He closed his eyes tight and lowered his head and stomped his foot, he was laughing so hard.

"Ha! No. No. No. He's our business manager, and he's really good at it. He gets us good deals from the vendors and even from the insurance company, with being so entertaining and how personable he is — and the way he never sits down, he gets more done in a day than the rest of us would in a week, it seems like."

Ever so gently, ever so slowly, she continued to draw out his personality by encouraging him to talk about his work.

Ever so gradually, he participated more and more in the conversation.

After a few hours, he seemed almost normal. Almost warm. Almost alive.

Hope blossomed in Amber's heart. Here alone with her, he was himself again and not that sycophantic zombie following after Sulis. Maybe he would see his way out of her influence. Maybe Amber would get her second chance with him after all, despite the difficulty and all the weirdness. She nourished the hope. She let it convince her things would be okay, that everything would work out.

Until Sulis barged in.

The perfectly coiffed blonde stormed over and

grabbed Tomas's hand, pulling him to her and whispering in his ear, the whole time staring daggers at Amber.

Immediately, Tomas zombied up again.

The twinkle left his eyes.

The sense of camaraderie they'd been sharing disappeared — worse, all signs of intelligence or even autonomy left his whole countenance. He was like a walking rag doll. Blank. Empty.

Without saying anything, Sulis dragged him away, casting a furious glance at Amber behind her.

Cursing, Amber threw her tools down and left the room to follow them.

Còig (5)

Amber ran quite a ways down the carven stone corridors lit by strings of white Christmas lights, thinking to at least hear Tomas and Sulis if not see them after rounding each corner. But it was as if the living rock walls of the ancient underground castle had swallowed them up.

She finally had to admit that Sulis had won this round. She couldn't find them.

So she sought out Kelsey instead, and joined her and Tavish for lunch at the crew's lunch truck. Amber was dying to tell them she had connected with Tomas again and Sulis had ruined it, but with all the people around, they could only talk shop. They did so for several hours, with Amber supplying mostly answers and Kelsey asking a thousand questions. And then Kelsey excused herself and Tavish to do some errand or other, and Amber went back to her room with the tree carved in the floor and worked, alone.

Just after sunset as everyone was headed back to their trailers, Amber was still alone when she saw Sulis walking out in the grassy field in a white robe, singing.

Amber headed off into the grass to follow the druidess.

Sulis headed toward the cliffs.

Amber followed, growing more and more curious what the woman would do when she got there. Did she know Amber was following? Did she hope to make Amber fall off the cliff the way her fellow druid had failed to?

Yeah, Sulis knew Amber was following, because she waited at the edge of the cliff. She had no other reason to do that. But Amber wasn't sure how Sulis knew she was coming. She was hiding under a bushy tree, peering through some branches, so she should have been invisible from over there on the cliff. Oh well.

Wait, what!

Amber rubbed her eyes.

Sulis was going over the edge of the cliff.

Amber took off running as fast as she could.

"Wait! I don't mean to hurt you. I just want to tell you to release whatever unnatural hold you have on Tomas. Don't jump. We can work this out. It's not too late!"

But Sulis only laughed and slowly lowered herself over the cliff on a rope that must've been hidden from Amber's view.

Sure enough, when Amber got to the cliff, she noticed a rope ladder that was tied to a tree stump. Taking a deep breath and letting it out slowly, she took hold of the top rung and tugged on it, unsure if it was sturdy even after watching Sulis go down it.

Don't be a coward, she told herself. However else the two of you are different — which is pretty much in everything down to the smallest detail — you look like you weigh about the same.

Before she could lose her nerve, she planted her foot on a lower rung and swung her butt over the edge of the cliff. Whoa, looking down was a mistake. There were the waves crashing violently against the rocks.

Heart beating rapidly, Amber made herself put one foot down, then the other, then both hands — until she saw a cave there in the side of the sea cliff.

Wow.

She stepped off the rope ladder into a tunnel. This one was down deeper than those she and Kelsey had been working on, but the failing sunlight penetrated the cave somehow up ahead, so it wasn't dark.

Taking confidence from this, she entered the cave, keeping on guard in case Sulis jumped out at her. This was a natural cave, rough and dirty, not a carved out corridor — though her mind told her it would connect to the network of those eventually, or why would there be a ladder to it.

After a few seconds, it was tempting to call out Sulis's name, it seemed so desolate down here. At least it didn't stink like some of the ruins where she'd worked. These cliffs under Dunskey Castle were open to the ocean air, so there was a pleasant nautical scent.

Oh, she could hear footsteps up ahead, now that she was deeper into the tunnel and out of earshot of the waves.

Speeding up to a run, Amber followed the sound of Sulis's footsteps through ancient rooms full of secrets. She longed to linger down here, exploring. Nothing was as she expected it to be in a castle. This was old. A relic from a much different time. The Iron Age, Kelsey had said.

Sulis led her on a merry chase up one level and down the next, around this bend and over that set of stairs. Amber ran down a hallway where she'd thought she heard Sulis's footsteps only to hit a dead-end.

When she stopped to turn around, Amber reasoned that she must've run really fast down that particular hallway, because she felt so dizzy she had to stop and put her hands on her knees and wait for the vertigo to pass.

It took an unusually long time.

It took so long that once she had recovered, she could no longer hear Sulis's footsteps.

Amber crept down to the beginning of that dead-end corridor and looked around, listening. Still no sound of Sulis, but at least she was pretty sure she knew where she was now. Checking on her theory, she walked toward her and Kelsey's work area.

Well that was strange. She was sure this was the area where the big table should be with all the artifacts they were cataloguing and everybody's pouches of tools, but someone had turned out the lights. She got out her phone to use as a flashlight. Maybe this wasn't it after all. But it sure seemed to be. There was the crevice which looked like a dog. And that was the spot she was always having to duck sideways to miss as she made the last turn into the room.

Well, maybe everybody had moved their things out while she was chasing Sulis?

Including the lights?

What the heck was going on? Kelsey would know. Amber went over near one of the small drafty side caves where she had used her phone this morning successfully.

But now there was no signal.

Kelsey had better have a good reason why all their stuff had been moved — and where was it? Had Mr. Blair brought in yet more trailers?

Suddenly needing to know if her tools were still on the floor where she had thrown them, Amber headed over that way. But she stopped abruptly. The secret door to the room she had been working in two hours ago was closed. And there were cobwebs in front of it.

Goosebumps rose on the back of her neck and trailed down the backs of her arms.

She kept looking for the signal to re-connect as she walked toward the root cellar with the ladder that went up out the trap door. But the secret door at the end of that hallway was closed. It had never been closed before.

She had no idea how to open that door.

Panic rose in her chest. She hadn't had a panic attack since she was thirteen.

There had to be a logical explanation for why these doors were closed and why all their stuff was missing—

Tavish.

Tavish must be playing a practical joke on her.

It wasn't funny.

The anger she felt at him gave her the strength to turn around and retrace her steps back to the rope ladder. Only, it wasn't there.

Panic tried to take hold of her again, and fortunately, her therapist's advice for fighting panic twelve years ago came back to her. Slow, deep breaths. Think logically. Work on the trouble.

The deep breaths were the easiest part. She had them down. Thinking logically about all this, though? Maybe she'd better just skip to working on the trouble. But doing what?

Looking for a way out, that's what.

Maybe the rope ladder was there and had just drifted outside of the cave a bit. Maybe if she went to the opening and felt around outside, she would find it.

She got to the cave opening — high up over the crashing waves — and held on to a rock which jutted out of the cave wall while she reached out and felt around.

Puzzled at what she felt, she nonetheless pulled it inside to have a look.

It wasn't a rope ladder at all, but it was a rope. A single strand of rope that looked handmade.

She'd had enough, and she yelled up out of the cave mouth.

"Tavish! There's no way I'm climbing up with just this stupid flimsy old rope! Throw down the rope ladder. Right now! Do you hear me? I said throw down the rope ladder right now."

~*~

After yelling up the cliff for half an hour, Amber was seeing red. Tavish still hadn't come.

And maybe he expected her to repel up the side of the cliff with only the handmade rope as a safeguard against falling down onto the rocks, but she didn't feel up to that. She had barely made herself climb down the rope ladder. Climb up with just this rope? Nuh uh.

Tavish had told her on her first day that there was another entrance down a stairway that wasn't in use now because they were trying to preserve it. She hadn't seen that staircase in her wanderings today, but she had mostly been deeper than the first level, where a staircase would be. In most of the underground palace, the halls just slanted downward.

But in Kelsey's whirlwind tour in their dream, there had been a staircase up. Amber turned around to go back down the cave again.

As soon as she did, she saw Tomas coming toward her — wearing a kilt like Tavish's. A pleatit-each-time-you-put-it-on 'great kilt' like the ones they had worn to the Renaissance Faire. He looked wonderfully familiar in it. And sexy.

She felt so confused in the moment that her tongue was tied, a rarity for Amber. Usually she talked way more than was good for her. But right now, Tavish was playing this trick on her, and she felt inadequate to climb up a rope, and Sulis had led her down here and then abandoned her, and now Tomas seemed to be playing along with this part of the joke.

How stupid could she be?

Somehow, Tomas had been the one person she thought she could trust, even more than Kelsey. But now he had proven otherwise by showing up in this kilt and being part of this stupid joke. She was angry and frustrated and sad and lonely.

Considering he'd been a zombie most of the time she'd seen him lately, Amber was surprised when Tomas had no qualms at all about how he felt.

He yelled at her, making her jump.

"What are you doing here in modern clothing?"

Finally settling on feeling defeated, Amber slumped down and sat on the cold stone cave floor.

"Tomas, I don't know what game this is, but I'm not playing."

Surprising her again, he took her by the arm and pulled her up, then tugged her down the hallway.

"I can't believe you're doing this, Amber. You

don't even know how serious this is, do you? Of course not. You just got here. Why did you have to do this? Sulis is so pissed, I think she might even... I don't know what she's going to do, but it's not going to be good. Just let me get you out of here, okay?"

It had felt wonderful when he first took her arm, and it wasn't half bad even now, with him tugging her along as if she were a child. He seemed oblivious to the effect it was having on her, however. Didn't chemistry work both ways? If she was feeling chemistry, wasn't he feeling it too?

She took a deep breath and let it out, surprised to find that she really didn't need to. Her anxiety had disappeared as soon as he showed up — even though he had yelled at her.

Resigned to being tugged by the arm, Amber just followed along. At least Tomas seemed to know where he was going. She just stayed quiet, hoping he really would get her out of here.

But no such luck.

Tomas continued this weird game they were playing, although at least his yelling had gradually wound down, and now he was just talking.

"I'm going to take you to the travel spot. You need to stay there while I go get Tavish, okay?"

Just play along. Get the game over with.

"Okay."

He took her back to that room where the table should have been with all their stuff, and planted her against the wall at a T intersection of the corridors.

"Okay, I'm going to get Tavish so he can take you home. Wait right here."

He looked her in the eyes when he said to wait right here — and took her breath away.

She saw deep concern for her in his eyes.

"Yeah, okay, I'll wait right here."

She watched him run back toward the staircase, his kilt swishing in a pleasing way. And she did wait there. But while she was waiting, a strange song came to her ears. It was barely audible, but pleasing. Just when she was starting to wonder again what was going on and where everything had gone, the music changed.

It was singing, she realized. Soft, beautiful singing in a woman's voice. She couldn't understand the words, but the song called out to her nonetheless in feelings that her mind translated for her.

"Follow me. Follow me to beauty. Follow me to happiness. Follow me to the answer to all of your dreams."

The song just hinted of this at first, but the longer she listened, the louder it got — and the more insistent. She found herself getting up and taking a few steps forward, the song was so compelling.

"The worries of your heart will be answered. An end to all your yearning is near. Come, taste the freedom."

But it was more than just these promises. The song somehow made her see visions of green fields with butterflies fluttering above them, and glittering waterfalls with fairies dancing in the mist. Vaguely, she was aware that she was wandering through the underground castle, but she was going a way she hadn't gone before. She didn't worry about it. She was following the promise of the song, and it kept getting brighter and more hopeful by the minute.

"Come dance with your love up in the sunlight. Come out of these caves in this darkness into the glorious day."

In the back of her mind, her logical reasoning protested that the sun had just set and it was night time now, but she ignored this still soft voice. Because the promise was so strong, so alluring.

"You can have everything you desire if you only follow. Come with me on a journey into the best places you'll ever see."

Already she was seeing things she'd never seen before. Oh, she passed through the grand throne room Kelsey had told her about, with the golden throne. It did look heavy. Vaguely, she wondered how Kelsey and Tavish and all the crew would ever get it out of there. And she passed through several secret doors that hadn't been open before — and again she wondered who had done the secret combination of movements of bricks to open them. She knew she hadn't.

But it really didn't matter. Nothing mattered except following the song that was going to bring her back to Tomas. It was going to join the two of them in all the ways that she was dreaming of. It was going to make them happy together for the rest of their lives.

Her feet moved faster now. She was running through the decorated stone corridors. She had put her phone in her pocket when she was looking for the rope ladder, but a twinkly fairy light guided her steps and didn't let her trip.

Way back in the background of her mind, she noticed that the wall and floor carvings here weren't so debris-filled as the ones she'd been clearing. The tiniest part of her mind wondered why that was — but the greater part dismissed it.

She could see the stairs now, the stairs Tavish and told her about, that she had been wondering about. There was nothing fancy about them, so why weren't they being used? They didn't appear to need preserving.

This also was dismissed. The song was full blast now. The source of the song was at the top of the stairs, waiting for her along with all the promises of the song — everything she ever wanted.

She ran up the stairs two at a time, impatient to get to where the promises waited. Bursting out into the cloudy light of a typical dreary Scottish day, she smiled and looked around for Tomas.

She didn't see him, but the song told her where she would find him.

"Come over here to the edge of the cliff."

She couldn't get there fast enough. Even though it was difficult to run in her Doc Martens, she did run. Over the grass and stones. Across the path she had taken toward Port Patrick the night before. Right up to the edge of the cliff she ran, and stayed there, gazing at the waves as they dashed against the jagged sharp rocks far below.

"Are not the waves gallant?" asked the song which still hummed in her ear with a melodious beauty surpassed by nothing she ever imagined. "Are they not strong and beautiful, the way they dash with such purpose — and that magnificent sound?"

In Amber's imagination, the song was now a beautiful fairy who had come to grant all of her secret wishes. So Amber nodded yes in response to the fairy's question. For the waves were indeed majestic and noble, deserving a great strong purpose. It was nearly impossible to tear her gaze away from them.

When she had been there a minute or so, watching the waves, she began to yearn for them. To want them to embrace her. For their strength to carry her with their purpose.

At that point, the song changed again. It became even more beautiful, with lovely notes that carried on the wind and reminded her of the ocean, the way they drifted up and down so predictably and so comfortingly.

"The gallant waves wait to take you to your own personal paradise. All you need do is go to them. Now."

Realizing this was her cue, that she was meant to do this and it would be the answer to all of her wishes, Amber raised her foot to step off the cliff.

Sia (6)

Before Amber fell off the cliff into the welcoming waves, a hand snatched her arm and pulled her back. Irritated, she turned, ready to chew the person out, whoever it was.

But it was Kelsey. Since lunch, she had changed into a floor-length plaid overdress in blues and browns with a bit of yellow. Under that was an extra floor-length skirt in plain brown. The big billowing sleeves of her linen blouse were light blue.

Her stricken brown eyes searched Amber, and when Kelsey spoke, it was in Gaelic.

"Whatever are ye doing, Amber, trying tae give us the vapors? How did ye get here, and why didn't ye change clothes first?"

Even as she listened to Kelsey, Amber could still hear the song, but it was fading. Desperate to get what she wanted, Amber fought against Kelsey's hold, fought to go over the cliff after all. She could still see the waves down there, waiting to welcome her. Just a few more inches, and she would join them.

But another hand took hold of her other arm and yanked her away from the cliff. Oddly, this second person stopped and fell, but Kelsey caught the second person.

This new person — also a woman, it turned out — spoke to Kelsey, also in Gaelic. What was up with these people and their costumes and their old-fashioned language? What kind of game was this?

"Naught much. She will be at oor wedding. Nevertheless, we need tae get her inside."

"Aye, howsoever for now, just put yer cloak aroond her."

The other woman laughed. Laughed. At a time like this. Kelsey and her friend must still be playing Tavish and Tomas's game. Great. For a moment, Amber regretted ever leaving the Mexican dig site. Her old friends were strange to her, and she felt more alone than ever. But...

Now that she was away from the cliff and these women were talking...

What was she doing here?

Oh yeah. There had been that song... It was gone now.

She stopped fighting against them and relaxed. Kelsey was her friend. She wasn't going to hurt her. Why was she fighting against her? The idea of walking off the cliff now filled her with horror instead of... Why she been walking off the cliff, again?

Meanwhile, Kelsey's friend had removed her cloak and was arranging it over Amber's shoulders, where she fastened it with her brooch. She looked at Kelsey and grinned.

"We will take ye inside and find ye some aught tae wear, but in the meantime ye will be fine sae long as ye keep this cloak about ye."

Amber looked at the woman. Also dressed in a long plaid dress and a bell-sleeved linen blouse, she was tall and red haired and smiling with joy.

"Ah, ye must be Sasha."

Sasha nodded and smiled.

Amber studied her. She seemed to be a modern woman, but did she only understand Gaelic? Amber spoke to her in that language, which Tavish's parents had taught her at the fair.

"Hae I seen ye afore? Because ye look familiar."

Sasha laughed again.

"Wull if ye were a man and I wasna about tae be marrit — in the middle o planning my wedding ceremony right at this moment, as a matter o fact — I would tease ye and say some aught like 'only in yer dreams.'" She gave Amber a weird significant look, giving her the impression she should know something but didn't, and then shrugged and went on. "Howsoever, syne ye are na a man and I dinna feel like teasing ye, I shall just say nay, na really. 'Tis nice tae meet ye,

Amber. I hae heard a little about ye and all yer other faire friends ower the years. I lived with Kelsey during her studies. Did she tell ye?"

Amber didn't answer, because she couldn't get enough breath.

She was coming out of a daze and had only just noticed the huge very solid stone-on-stone castle that loomed next to them. In no way shape or form had that been there three hours ago when she followed Sulis over the cliff. There had only been the old tower house, which was much smaller than this... fortress.

Sasha and Kelsey turned to follow Amber's gaze at the castle, and then turned back to her.

Kelsey nodded.

"'Tis magnificent, aye?"

Still struggling to get enough breath because of the anxiety that now gripped her again, Amber wrinkled her brow at Kelsey and managed to squeak out a question.

"Magnificent? More like impossible! Where the 'check' did it come from?"

But Kelsey and Sasha weren't looking at Amber anymore. She followed the direction they were looking in.

Half a dozen kilted guards outfitted in leather armor, heavy handmade boots, and hundreds of pounds of weapons were headed their way. And Sasha and Kelsey were smiling at them.

The guards halted when they got to Amber and her friends. Their leader looked Amber over appreciatively but politely as he spoke to Kelsey.

"Wull now am I tae be supposing this is

another o yer clanswomen come tae market, Kelsey?"

Kelsey smiled at him and put her arm through Amber's arm.

"Aye, she is. Cormac, this is Amber. And afore ye ask, I dinna ken how long she will be staying. Amber, these are some o Laird Malcomb's brawest castle guards."

Amber tried to be polite and play along. She really did.

But this was all too much. What the heck?

First she almost stepped off the cliff — had seen the dashing waves beneath her with their foam coming up and known she was going to fall to her death — and now here was a whole castle that hadn't been there before — and guards straight out of Braveheart. The only thing missing was the blue face paint. The rational part of her mind said she would have to ask Kelsey about that later.

But most of her struggled to say something, anything, that would make sense in the situation.

But her lungs constricted until she was gasping for air. Black spots appeared before her eyes, and the next thing she knew, she was collapsing.

~*~

Amber woke up in a bed. It was very comfortable, and the covers were heavy and luxurious — handmade quilts, going by the stitches she felt with her fingers. She pulled the covers up over her head to go back to sleep. For some reason, she was stressed out. Yeah, best to go back to sleep before she remembered why.

But no such luck.

Kelsey's voice grabbed her attention and wouldn't let go, and Kelsey's hand pulled the covers down.

"Oh good, you're okay. It's safe to talk now. It's just us women. You can trust Sasha. The guys are waiting outside. We're all dying to know how you got here by yourself, and why didn't you change clothes first?"

Huh? This must be another persistent dream. Maybe if she sat up, she'd wake up more and things would be less confusing. Instead, she pulled the covers back over her head again.

"This has got to be a nightmare. Just let me go back to sleep so I can wake up again and have all this be over."

Kelsey pulled the covers down to Amber's waist.

"I wish this were a dream, because then I could manipulate things the way I wanted them, but it's not. We're really here in the fourteenth century, and you're really with us. I found some clothes you can change into, so that's less of a problem. But Amber, how did you get here? The only way the rest of us are able to time travel is with Tavish's ring. We're super curious to know how you managed it."

Amber put her elbows behind her and used them to help her sit up. As she did so, she noticed the stone block construction of the small but nicely appointed bedroom they were in. Its windows were skinny and tall, barely letting in any light, but it did have a warmly burning fireplace. More light came from candles in holders on the walls. Aside from the bed, there was just an armchair and a dresser with a pitcher and bowl on top of it.

Sasha was sitting in the armchair. She waved.

With a heavy sigh, Amber sat up in the bed and threw her legs over the side, waved back, then turned to Kelsey.

"I didn't get here by myself. Are you kidding? I had no idea. Sulis must have brought me here. She was wearing a white druid robe like you described, and she was singing out in the grass. I followed her down a rope ladder over the cliff into a cave that led to the underground castle, and she led me on a merry chase. She must have taken me back in time while she did so—"

"Did you get dizzy?"

"Yeah, really dizzy. But Kelsey, that's not the scariest part. Her song hypnotized me. It made me want to jump off the cliff."

Kelsey sat down on the bed next to Amber and hugged her, then jumped up and went and got a parcel Amber hadn't noticed before.

"Fortunately, we're apprenticed to a weaver here, and she likes to sew. There's lots of extra clothes lying around. They don't have sizes, but I think these will fit."

Amber got up and put the outfit on. It was much like Kelsey and Sasha's, only more green and yellow, less brown. While she changed, Kelsey and Sasha exchanged worried looks.

When she had finished dressing and adjusting,

Amber put her hands on both of their shoulders.

"Please, tell me what's going on. I always thought it would be fun if I could go back in time. Why are druids making me jump off cliffs?"

Kelsey furtively glanced at the door.

"How about if we let the guys come in so that Tavish can explain?"

Amber looked at the door too.

"Is Tomas out there?"

Kelsey nodded yes.

There wasn't a mirror in the room, or Amber would've been in front of it checking herself out. Not having that way to stall, she simply ran her fingers through her bed hair and then nodded yes in return.

Tomas was scowling at her when he came in, but it wasn't a strong scowl. His face looked more worried than angry.

"Why did you have to go and wander away from that spot? I got Tavish as quickly as I could, and we went back there and you were gone."

Kelsey appealed to Tavish with her eyes, and her boyfriend put his hand on his twin's arm.

"Let it go, okay? She's had a shock, and she fainted after nearly falling off a cliff."

Tomas opened his mouth to argue, but then he nodded up once and turned aside and crossed his arms.

Amber went over into his line of sight.

"What's going on, Tomas?"

And just like that, all the animation left his face. He got a glazed look in his eyes and didn't answer.

Kelsey gave Amber a significant look that said 'I told you Sulis put a spell on him.'

Tavish stepped forward and took Amber's arm, walking her away from Tomas.

"To make a long story short, our ancestor made a pledge to a druid a long time ago — well actually, it's in the future right now. Anyway, every fourth born son in our family has to serve the druids if he lives to be twenty-five. I'm the fourth born son, and I've been serving them for nearly six years—"

Amber cut in, gesturing back and forth between Tavish and Tomas.

"But your twenty-fifth birthday was only six months ago."

Tavish nodded.

"Yes, but I've been here — in the past — for six years on-and-off during those six months. No time passes back home while I'm here. This magic ring they gave me on my birthday is set that way." He held up his right hand and showed her a silver ring that looked uncannily like the rings Sasha and Kelsey wore on their right hands.

Now Tomas scowled at his brother.

"Would you quit bragging about your time traveling ring?"

Fortunately, Tavish didn't get in an argument with his brother, just swallowed and looked back at Amber, still holding his right hand up and showing her the ring.

"Ironically, the young druid known as Lachlan the Dark — the one who tried to run you off the cliff the other night — thinks he can hide here in the past. He's working on enslaving humans in our time, and we're trying to catch him. With this ring, I can take you back to our time if you want. But I think it's safer if we all stay here together."

Amber gasped.

"Uh, yeah. If he can go back and forth in time at will — and he's trying to enslave people in our time — and all of you are here? Yeah, I'm staying here with you."

Tomas spoke up again, with his eyebrows wrinkled at Amber.

"It appears that you can go back and forth in time at will by yourself too. What's up with that? And you never explained why you came here without changing into period clothing, putting us all in danger."

He had to be kidding.

Now it was Amber's turn to scowl at Tomas, and she did so with a dropped jaw.

"I didn't bring myself here. I had no idea anyone could. It was Sulis. She sang some sort of song and it hypnotized me and almost made me jump off the cliff."

At the mention of Sulis's name, something snapped in Tomas. All the anger drained out of him, and he slowly turned on his heel and left the room without saying a word.

Tavish went after his brother.

"I'm sorry," he said over his shoulder.

Amber stood there just taking one breath after the other, trying to calm down. What were they going to do about Tomas? Any mention of Sulis, and his brain went to mush. He had seemed almost normal up until she mentioned the druidess. Why had she done that?

Kelsey put a hand on Amber's shoulder. "Don't."

"Don't what?"

"Don't blame yourself. I can tell that's what you're doing. Remember this is Sulis's fault, not yours. Stay strong and positive. Remember, when all is said and done, you're probably the only one who can get through to him. He needs you, Amber."

Amber looked around the room.

"I want to go to bed. Is this where we're all staying while we're here? Because it seems pretty small for the four of us, and that's not including the witch with a B."

Kelsey gave Amber a minor smile at her little joke.

"No. In fact, Sulis has charmed Laird Malcomb into giving Tomas this castle room. Her magical powers are mighty, I can tell you — so long as she renews them out in nature daily. That's where she is right now. The laird's own nephew Seumas sleeps in the barracks along with Tavish and the other guards, while Tomas — a complete stranger to the laird — gets a room in the castle. But not only has she convinced the laird to give Tomas this room, she has also convinced him to put Tomas in charge of the underground castle guards, usurping part of the command of Laird Malcomb's elder nephew, Eileen's fiance Alfred, Seumas's older brother."

Amber made a face at Kelsey.

"Yeah, I didn't follow all that. I was with you so far as Tomas has this room in the castle when he really shouldn't, and Tomas is in charge of the guards of the underground palace when he shouldn't be. The rest of it was just a bunch of names I don't know."

Kelsey pursed her lips.

"Understandable. But you need to understand—"

Amber stretched her arms out and yawned.

"Can't we just go to our room at the inn and take a nap before I have to digest anything more today?"

Kelsey scrunched up her mouth.

"'Fraid not. This castle has spawned a town, but not a big enough town to support an inn. Nope. We're staying with Eileen, the weaver I'm apprenticed to, the one whose fiance Alfred is the rightful captain of the guard. And we're helping Eileen and Sasha plan their double wedding to Alfred and his brother Seumas."

Seachd (7)

That evening at the front of the great hall of the castle, Tomas set his pewter goblet down on the long wooden plank table and sighed with satisfaction, then turned to smile at his beautiful Sulis, who was seated in the highest place next to Laird Malcomb. For this feast was in her honor, as every feast rightfully should be.

Gazing into her sapphire eyes, he almost forgot what he was going to say. Oh yeah.

"I didna ken they had such good wine here, or I should hae come sooner."

She turned to the laird.

"Did ye hear that, Laird Malcomb? Tomas

gives his compliments on the wine. He's sae thoughtful, on top o being such a capable captain for yer dock guards."

The laird of the castle smiled the smile of a man truly pleased to have a lovely woman ministering to his needs. He was suitably grateful that she was arranging things so advantageously for him. Good on him, because she was saving him the trouble of finding a good dock guard captain such as himself.

But the laird's wife, seated on his other side, stared daggers at Sulis. Silly woman. Sulis was with Tomas. There was no need to defend her territory.

Heat rose in his body, from his shoulders up into his head.

No one should look at Sulis disrespectfully.

Not and get away with it.

As it was his duty to see that this didn't happen again, Tomas calmly put his hands on his chair arms in preparation to get up and go strangle the lady of the castle.

But beautiful Sulis put a hand on his shoulder, staying him. She put her mouth up against his ear and breathed into it, and calm washed through him. She stood up instead, addressing not only the laird, but the whole room of a hundred revelers whom the laird had gathered to do her honor, as was proper and only her due.

She raised her pewter goblet to them.

"Tae happy company!"

They all raised their tankards to her, for they were drinking ale at the lower tables.

"Tae happy company!"

They started to turn away, but she raised her hands up prettily and kept their attention with her lovely voice.

"I dae believe 'tis time the dancing began. I wish tae stretch my legs. Laird Malcomb, will ye tell the musicians tae start?"

Eager to please her — as he well should be — Laird Malcomb nodded at Sulis and then at the musicians, who were already assembling on their stage, brushing off food crumbs and still chewing. They knew they had better hop to it, or face her temper. Sulis had this place whipped into shape after only a week, she was so good at what she did.

Tomas turned to his goddess and smiled his congratulations for a successful feast in her honor.

She petted the back of his neck, and warm pleasure shot through him with the promise of what was to come later on that evening. And then she turned away from him, forcing him to focus on the room again.

He saw that Tavish and Kelsey's red-haired woman friend was one of the musicians, and she smiled with extra pleasure at being up on stage before she put her flute to her lips and played, dancing about to the beat. Her man Seumas stood in front of her clapping, and admiring her beauty, no doubt.

And then Sulis grabbed Tomas's hand and pulled him up and paraded with him proudly over to the dance area in the center of this great hall.

Tavish and Kelsey smiled and made as if to join their dance set, but Sulis turned her back on them. They should have known better. Tavish might be his brother, but he was only a common soldier, while he, Tomas, was captain of the dock guards.

The thought made him stand up straighter and swagger a little.

Instead of Tavish and Kelsey, all the most prominent people in the hall joined Tomas and Sulis's dance set. Well, the laird himself stayed at the table, presiding over the event, but his sons and their wives joined, along with his nephew Alfred — Tomas's fellow captain of the guard — and the nephew's fiancé, Eileen, the weaver who Kelsey was apprenticed to in this time.

And all of this honoring was only Sulis's due, to have the admiration and respect and homage of everyone.

She was so beautiful, his Sulis. So, so, so beautiful standing opposite him in the dance set clapping her hands prettily and smiling at everyone and nodding in time to the hammered dulcimer while the laird's eldest son and his wife swung down the line.

How nice it had been of the laird to give Sulis and him a room in his castle.

No, not nice, only what Sulis deserved.

Tomas smiled back at her, willing all of his gratitude to shine through.

She cozied up to him while the dance set allowed it and breathed her lovely warm juniper-scented breath on him while speaking softly to him.

"I see how ye look tae yer brother. Look again. Mayhap he's been coming here for years, but ye hae it better after only a week. He and his friend Seumas are just guards here. Their lasses are just a weaver's apprentice and a flute player. Ye, Tomas, hae a room here in the castle. Ye are a captain o the guard. Ye are important."

It all made him shiver in delight.

He danced proudly by her side the rest of the evening while his brother and his brother's friends watched enviously.

~*~

She was with him that night again in his castle room, and it was glorious.

He woke from a joyous sleep to see her dressing in her white linen robes. It was nearly sunrise, but they didn't have to get up yet. Breakfast wasn't for another hour.

Quite groggy, he fought with his lazy tongue in order to speak.

"Don't go."

"Aw, I must, my angel, but I'll come back."

"Take me with you."

She finished dressing and sat down on the bed, then leaned down and breathed in his ear again, making him tingle all over.

"I can't. Stay near the castle, in this time, until I return. Obey Laird Malcomb."

"I will."

She left, but he was no longer worried. Quite the opposite. She had something important to do out there in the woods in her white robe. What she needed to do was the priority. She would return and be with him again, and only that mattered.

He thought of her pretty face and lovely body as he gave himself a sponge bath with water from the pitcher on top of the dresser. He thought of her silky spun-gold hair as he dressed for the day in his kilt and humongous-sleeved linen shirt, plaid blanket wrap, and heavy boots. Her birdsong voice was on his mind while he went down the stairs toward the great hall to break his night's fast.

He sat down and was served a plate full of fried eggs, ham, and baked beans. There was a sturdy mug of ale to go with it. He was happily tucking in when someone sat next to him and plunked down a plate of self-serve food. Not a resident of the castle, then.

He looked up with the amount of condescension in his face that Sulis had encouraged. She'd said he mustn't allow his inferiors any room to question him or doubt him — that he must be superior at all times around those he was in charge of — namely, the underground castle guards.

He didn't know them all yet, and so he had to be that way with all the guards. And since he didn't know who was a guard and who was just a craftsman at the castle on an errand, he had to be that way with everyone.

Logic.

Sulis was teaching him, and he was grateful.

But he turned his head and saw not a

stranger, but his brother Tavish. Well, Tavish was one of the guards. And he'd done his duty in the underground castle before. So...

"What are ye doing here at the castle, Tavish? Should na ye be eating wherever it is the barracks guards eat?"

Tavish raised his eyebrows.

"Ye hae na been paying attention. This is where we lowly barracks guards eat, Captain."

He said 'Captain' as if it were a dirty word, but he said it. Tomas would let that go. For now.

"Well, ye should na be sitting next tae me, ye ken? I've got tae keep up appearances. Make sure the men ken my station." He looked over at another table where some men were gathered together. "Ye should go sit with them."

Tavish pursed his lips and made an angry face and shook his head. And lowered his voice to a hiss.

"If ye were na my brother... But ye are. Still and all, I care about ye. Ye hae been acting sae different syne this Sulis came intae yer life. It isna flattering for ye, Tomas. Dae ye na see that? Should ye na be in charge o yerself?"

His brother's words made Tomas's jaw and fists clench.

"And if ye were na my brother... but ye are, and sae ye shall live. But dinna sit at my table again. And ye are na tae speak with me till I hae spoken tae ye. And dinna speak o Sulis in that manner. Is that clear?"

Tavish didn't answer. He just got up, grabbed his food, and stomped over to the other table.

Once there, however, he smiled and laughed with his fellow guards while they ate together.

The base of Tomas's pewter tankard made a dent in the wooden table when he put it down, causing it to spill his ale all over. Some splashed on him.

Cursing and brushing himself off, he jumped up to go back to his room.

"Ye there! Coome and clean up this mess at once."

Tavish could be civil and even jovial with these strangers from another time, but he couldn't give his own brother the respect due his station? Who needed him. Kelsey would probably see how much trouble he was soon and leave him. It wasn't like they were married or anything. Why had his brother even let her get close to him?

And there it was.

A vision of Amber swam before Tomas, the way she had been in that room inside his new domain: the underground palace. Her amber eyes were soft and affectionate whenever she looked at him, and her face appealed to him every time their eyes met.

What was she doing here at this site, let alone here in the past? Didn't she remember they couldn't be together?

Wait.

Tavish and Kelsey weren't supposed to be a couple anymore, either. Every time he saw them together, something inside him shuddered in fear. He and Tavish had a good reason for staying away from Kelsey and Amber.

He didn't want Amber in his life anymore. For her own good. He... He'd had a good reason for leaving her. He couldn't put his finger on it right now, but it was a really good reason. He knew that. Why couldn't he remember?

Anyway, he had walked away from her. He had left her seven years ago without even saying goodbye. It had hurt him, but he had known it was the right thing to do. It had been the right thing, hadn't it? Yes. Yes, he felt assured it had. And now she was aware that he had a new girlfriend.

Why was she always coming into his thoughts like this? She didn't have to walk in front of him while he was dancing with Sulis and come up for wine at the same time as he did. She really shouldn't look into his eyes as if she were searching for a lost part of herself.

Well, she wasn't doing that last thing right now anywhere but in his imagination.

But she shouldn't be here.

Even though nothing else she was doing was wrong.

Her being here distracted him, and he had important things to do here at the castle for Laird Malcomb. He was the captain of the underground guard now, and he shouldn't be distracted. Not even by a dark-haired beauty who sometimes brought back memories of a love so strong, he had been willing to give her up for her own good.

Tomas had just finished changing into fresh clothes when Sulis came in, smelling of the woods.

He was so glad to see her, he ran over and hugged her tight.

"Why did you have to go out to the woods alone? Something might have happened to you. You should let me go along to protect you. You—"

But Sulis kissed him then, a breathy wet kiss that started at his ear and worked its way around to his mouth. Fireworks went off in his mind, and the world narrowed down to just her lips on his, she was that good a kisser. As soon as she was done kissing him, he would ask her...

What had he been wondering about?

Oh, who cared? Being with Sulis was bliss. He should enjoy her.

Ochd (8)

Amber woke up in the throne room of the underground palace and gasped when she felt the huge golden throne beneath her and looked down to see that she was wearing a crimson gown made entirely out of handmade linen lace. There was weight on top of her head. She reached up and grabbed something, then lowered it down so she could see. It was an ornate golden crown made from many strands of gold woven into Celtic knot shapes.

A woman giggled from the other side of the hall.

"Don't look so shocked. Just pinch yourself,

hint hint."

Pinch herself?

Oh yeah.

She looked up to see Kelsey and Sasha dressed equally as beautifully in handmade lace gowns, only theirs were blue and green.

"So this is a dream." Amber smiled appreciatively and nodded. "It's a good one. Do you plan on wearing a gown like that at your wedding?"

Sasha moved gracefully in her green dress as if she were dancing with Seumas the way she had the night before.

"Nah, they just get married in their regular clothes in this time period, so unfortunately I won't have a special wedding dress. We come here often in our dreams. It's a much easier way for her to show us around. You could have danced last night too, Amber. That one guard Cormac was really anxious to dance with you. All you would have had to do was smile at him, and he would have asked you."

Amber gave Kelsey a look that said 'Tell her what's going on, because I haven't the patience to and will end up being rude about it. You know me.'

Kelsey nodded then turned to her new friend.

"Amber's Tomas's ex-girlfriend, and we think if anyone can get Tomas away from Sulis, it'll be her—"

Impatient now with Kelsey's explanation, Amber threw her head back to look at the carvings in the ceiling—and get the other two women's attention.

"It's maddening, this assignment you've given me, Kelsey. It's really hard not being with him and yet hoping that I can be, you know? Especially since making him jealous is out of the question. I don't have a clue how else to get a guy back."

Sasha gave her a puzzled look.

"Why not make him jealous?"

Amber closed her eyes to try and escape from some of the pain of thinking about Tomas with that blank look on his face — or even worse, looking at Sulis as if she were a goddess — but that just made it all the more vivid in her memory.

"Because he's too broken already, by Sulis's machinations. I'm going to have to draw him out little by little until he remembers me again, and I don't even know if I get to keep him once I do that, she has him so messed up. This is the hardest thing I've ever done."

Kelsey gave her a determined face.

"He's worth it though , isn't he."

Sighing, Amber shook her head yes slowly.

"Of course he is."

This was getting too heavy. Time to think about superficial things for a while. Amber stood from the huge throne and found that she was wearing strange sandals made of rope. They were not the most comfortable things, but they were interesting.

She looked quizzically at Sasha.

"If there aren't any special clothes to prepare,

then why is it taking so long to plan this wedding?"

Sasha and Kelsey shared a conspiratorial look, but kept their mouths shut.

Amber threw her hands up.

"Out with it."

Sasha put her palms forward.

"Okay. Remember how I fell when I first touched you, out there on the cliffs?"

"How could I ever forget?"

"Well, I had a vision of you at my wedding, and you were fine, not a scratch on you. Tomas, too. My visions always come true, so we know that as long as we keep putting the wedding off, this Lachlan character won't be able to catch you, or at least he won't hurt you."

Amber looked at Kelsey for confirmation, and her friend gave her a playfully guilty look.

Sasha ran her hand down her long flowing red hair while she continued explaining the plan she and Kelsey had apparently made without Amber.

"Everyone who knows about time travel except Tomas—me, Seumas, Kelsey, and Tavish—knows you're safe. And Kelsey thinks we can use that to help snap Tomas out of the funk Sulis has him in. His urge to protect you is really strong. I was skeptical, but now I think it'll work."

Amber didn't want to think about that right now. It was too much on top of all this time travel stuff, so she gestured around at the throne room.

"Sulis lured me through here on her wild

goose chase. But it didn't seem this new — well, I guess it did happen eight hundred years from now, but—"

Kelsey nodded quickly and waved off Amber's puzzlement in a promise to explain.

"Yeah, no, you're right. This lower part of the underground palace is thousands of years old. The dream memories I have of it are from when it was new. Tavish and I came down here into this throne room after finding it through the dreams of an evil old druid named Brian. He must have time traveled back here during the Iron Age, when the Celts reigned here and raided the blue-painted Picts, whose kingdom was the eastern half of what is now Scotland."

The Celts! They were all anyone had talked of at faire. Celtic knots. Celtic warfare. Celtic culture. How exciting to actually go back to their age and see how they lived. She would be the envy of all her old friends. They would hang on her every word.

"I've heard all about the Celts, of course, but you said something about blue painted Picts? I meant to ask you about that when I saw those guards straight out of Braveheart earlier. They had everything except the blue face paint Mel Gibson wore in the movie."

Kelsey laughed. So did Sasha.

"Just because it's in a movie doesn't mean it's authentic. It was the Picts who painted themselves blue with woad, not the Celts."

And then Amber jumped, because Kelsey gestured, and for a moment they were out in a field of battle watching Roman soldiers get jumped by naked people painted blue with odd blue designs all over their bodies. And then they were back inside the underground palace.

Amber gave Kelsey a huge grin.

"Does this Brian still know how to get there? Can he take us?"

Kelsey shivered.

"Ew, no. The man was evil, Amber. He's dead now."

Amber's face fell.

Kelsey snickered at her.

"But I still have all of his dreams in my memory, so I can show you some more sometime."

Amber nodded vigorously, still with that huge grin on her face.

Kelsey laughed at her.

"Tonight I'm going to show you the entire Celtic underground palace, so that you won't get lost again. That B-witch may be able to humiliate us at grand feasts held in her honor, but never again is she going to make any of us get lost inside our own dig site."

Amber jumped up off the stone counter she was leaning on and followed Kelsey and Sasha down the corridor. But as they walked, she just couldn't help hashing over last night's feast.

"Maybe it's sour grapes on my part because Sulis is with Tomas now, but I thought she was the biggest B-witch ever last night."

Sasha made a cutting gesture with her hand.

"She was unconscionable, no sour grapes

about it. I could see everything from up on the stage. It's the custom to form new sets for each new dance, but whenever others tried to form up with Malcomb's sons, Sulis stepped on their toes or stared daggers at them so they would back off. She even shoved this one couple out of her way so she could continue monopolizing the spotlight."

Kelsey put her arm over Sasha's shoulders.

"I saw how rude she was to Seumas."

Sasha looked at something down at the end of the large hollowed-out stone hallway while she sighed deeply.

"It broke my heart, seeing his brother shun him like that. It was all her doing, of course. I think I'll refrain from playing at any more feasts while she's here. I could have warned him if I hadn't been playing. But Kelsey, if she's here during our wedding…"

Kelsey gave Sasha a quick sideways hug.

"No way. We are not going to let Sulis ruin your wedding. She puts on those white linen robes and goes out in the woods every chance she gets, have you noticed?"

Sasha nodded.

"We'll just stall until she feels her powers fading and needs to go out there, is all. You'll play the flute, and you can get the other musicians to play. Maybe even have dancing. Let her dance awhile. She seems to like that. It'll be worth it in order to get her out of the picture for the actual wedding ceremony."

Sasha laughed a little, but she also brushed a

tear away.

"I think that may actually work. Thanks. I feel better."

With that, all three women linked arms — and then Kelsey slowly floated them around the entire underground palace until Amber knew every inch of it. She still didn't know how to open the secret doors, though. Kelsey just made them float right through those.

"We would teach you how to open these doors if it were simple, Amber. But it isn't. It took us years of study not really aimed at this — or so we thought — in order to open them, so you'll just have to take one of us along whenever you explore down here."

Amber scoffed.

"Wish I could have had you down here when B-witch brought me through the cave off the cliff down the rope ladder."

Kelsey dropped their linked arms and side hugged Amber.

"She brought you in that way? I'm so sorry — but I'm impressed you were able to make it."

Amber hugged her friend back.

"That's how pissed off I was. It made me stronger. Thinking about it now makes me feel strong enough to chew rocks."

Kelsey patted Amber's shoulder.

"Here in the dream, you could chew rocks, but let's not and say we did."

At that, Amber laughed the tiniest bit.

"Deal." But then her anger took over again. "Sulis has some nerve, showing up here at our dig site and taking over — and using Tomas against us."

Kelsey growled a little.

"I know. She's gotten him installed here so that she can recruit more of her zombie slaves out of his guards and then have them loot everything out of here before we even get a chance. But you know that's not the worst of it. What she's doing to Tomas is. It isn't really him doting over her like that. She has him charmed but good. His real personality comes out every once in a while. I know you've seen it. Tavish has too, but for some reason the sight of his brother makes Tomas so furious that Tavish can't get through to him."

Amber took a deep breath and let it out as the three of them floated down the corridor past rooms that nearly sparkled in their cleanliness under the light of many torches.

"Aren't there ever any people in here in this Brian the Druid's dreams? It's really eerie without people."

Kelsey gave Amber a 'let's be frank' look.

"At first, I used to have the people in the dream with me. They are interesting, and maybe some time when one of us isn't in urgent need of knowing where everything is, I'll let you see the people too. But they're so distracting. We'd spend our whole time watching all of their fascinating rituals."

Sasha gave Kelsey a hopeful look at that.

Kelsey nodded at her, and the two of them might as well have been rubbing their hands together, they looked so eager to study the Celts.

Amber took Kelsey's hand and squeezed it.

"This was a good idea. I'm glad to know my way around. You're right, we shouldn't let her have any advantage on our own turf. And I hereby declare this underground Celtic palace ours."

The place was magnificent, and quite a bit larger than Amber had first guessed, going down four levels before it reached the sea. She lost count of how many secret doors they passed through in order to get that far down, and then they went up by a different route, passing through even more and taking several flights of stairs. But she thought that as long as it didn't involve opening any secret doors, she could now find her way out no matter where she was in the underground castle.

And the night's adventure had to end sometime.

Sasha was especially pale in the light of all the torches, and her face looked especially mournful.

"Well, we'd better get home and go to bed."

Amber jumped in before Kelsey could say anything.

"Aw, can't we stay a little longer? This is fun, and you have to admit, life in the waking world is trying right now, dealing with Sulis."

Gently shaking her head no, Kelsey took Amber and Sasha's hands, and then all three of them became ghostlike and floated straight up through four layers of rock corridors until they were on the surface, standing on the wet grass in their bare feet under a sky that held so many stars, it was almost solid light.

Kelsey gave it a moment before she spoke and broke the peacefulness.

"No, we don't really get rest while I'm manipulating our dreams. Sasha's right, we have to go back to our bodies and allow them to rest."

Amber squeezed Kelsey's hand.

"Well at least tomorrow you can show me the upper castle in the real daylight."

But Sasha put a hand on Amber's arm.

"We were going to do that, but Seumas thinks it's too dangerous for us to let Lachlan run around without watching where he's going... Amber, we want Tomas to think Lachlan is after you in particular, so that his protectiveness is aroused. He'll see otherwise if you come with us, so you're going to stay and help Eileen in the weaver shop tomorrow while we're out."

Amber opened her mouth to speak, but what could she say really?

Kelsey put a hand on Amber's back.

"I'm sorry. I know that's not too exciting. You can have a tour of the castle and the town the next day, okay?"

Sasha gave a little laugh.

"It won't be all bad. Wait until you meet Eileen's daughter Deirdre. Heh! She's six years old going on sixty. She'll keep you entertained."

~*~

Amber woke up with a tiny pair of blue eyes a foot from her face, staring at her unblinking.

"A good morning tae ye. My name is Amber,

and some aught tells me ye are Deirdre."

The blue eyes widened.

"What is it that tells ye?"

Amber smiled at the little cherub of a girl.

"I would say a little birdie telt me, but ye ken that would be a lie, dae ye na?"

Deirdre's nose scrunched up, and she backed away and put her hands on her hips.

"Dinna be silly. Little birds dinna talk. I thought... wull, never mind what I thought. If ye are gaun'ae come help us in the weaver shop today, then ye had better get up and eat yer parritch. Maw has already left with the bairns. She left me tae look after ye." Deirdre gave Amber a quick once-over. "I daresay ye dinna ken any better than Sasha how we live here, dae ye?"

Wow, Sasha wasn't kidding.

"I reckon I ken how tae eat parritch."

~*~

Eileen smiled when her daughter dragged Amber into the weaver shop.

"Thank ye for watching ower my new apprentice, Deirdre. Sìle needs ye tae look after her now, please."

Amber expected Deirdre to put up a fuss, but to her amazement, the little girl went right over to where her baby sister was playing with some fist-sized wooden spools and took over supervising her, modulating her voice to sound somewhat like their mother's.

"There's a good lass. Are ye playing nice, now?"

Eileen beckoned Amber over into the far corner of the shop, where piles of burlap bags were stacked up against the wall.

"Ye are in luck. Kelsey has been helping me pound flax intae thread, and 'tis a tedious task." She gestured over at the man who was weaving on a huge loom between them and Deirdre. "Howsoever, Fergus just traded for all o this raw wool, sae we get tae spin it intae yarn instead. Much easier."

Amber looked at the spinning wheel dubiously.

Eileen bit her thumb and smiled around it for a moment before saying anything.

"'Tis na sae daunting as all that. I shall feed the wool intae the groove here. All ye need dae is keep the wheel spinning."

It took a few minutes, but Amber got the hang of spinning the wheel. Because it was tedious, repetitive, boring work, and Sasha and Kelsey had spoken of Eileen like she was one of them, soon Amber found herself sharing what was on her mind.

She spoke in hushed tones so that the men across the room wouldn't hear.

"Hae ye noticed aught strange about Tomas?"

"Plenty, and Alfred has noticed as wull. I hear about it daily. Alfred is having tae train Tomas in how tae captain the guards. A man that inexperienced should na be in command, says Alfred."

"But Laird Malcomb would be the one tae dae some aught about that, aye?"

"Aye, howsoever, if ye ask me, the

strangeness is in Sulis. She has that Tomas bewitched, and mayhap Laird Malcomb as wull."

They worked for a while in silence, and then Eileen made a noise and put her finger in her mouth.

Amber jumped up.

"Dinna ye hae a thimble I can get for ye?"

Eileen laughed.

"I ken ye are na ower enchanted by the work we dae here."

Amber laughed too.

"Daes it show that much?"

"Aye. But I hae good news for ye. I hae lost my thimble, and I dae think ye should go and get me another."

Amber knew her face had brightened an obvious amount because Eileen's smile grew larger as she dug in her pouch for some money and handed it to her.

"I buy whatsoever I can from Joanna the Tinker, a widow who needs all the help we can give tae her. The booth is just doon the way there—"

Dierdre came running over.

"Canna I show her please Maw?"

Amber shrugged when Eileen looked for her opinion on this idea.

Eileen gave Dierdre a serious look.

"Verra wull, howsoever, ye must dae as Amber tells ye."

Dierdre nodded somberly and then looked up at Amber.

"I will." And then she grabbed Amber's hand

and tugged her toward the door. "Let's go!"

~*~

Dierdre tugged Amber to a small market table in a group of other small tables, where a bunch of older women — could they all be widows? That was so sad. — sat in a haphazard circle mending shirts or darning socks while they talked and waited for customers who needed something mended or washed.

Amber had just bought the thimble and was thanking Joanna when Sulis turned the corner and stopped almost on top of her.

Tomas followed close behind Sulis, holding everything she had bought. He had a bolt of cloth in one arm and a bunch of do-dads in his other arm and wore three of her hats on his head as he walked along the street like a zombie with his eyes not showing any life.

Feeling horrible for him, Amber rounded on Sulis.

"How dare ye turn such a smart and vibrant man intae such a drone and call it love?"

Sulis took a haughty stance and crossed her arms over her ample chest and raised her chin up high before she spoke in a loud voice so that everyone nearby could hear her and didn't have a choice but to listen.

"Move on tae some poor shop where ye can trade for what ye need, Amber, because I ken for a clean fact ye don't hae any money tae pay for anything. Ye are just wasting the time o these craftsmen, hanging about and staring at everything with longing. Move aside and let those o us who can afford the goods shop here."

Amber made a show of looking about.

"There are nay craftsmen tae be seen anywhere close by, only widows. Who are beneath yer notice, I see."

Sulis just stood there looking down her nose at Amber, plainly expecting her to cower before her magnificence and clear away.

But Joanna stood from her comfortable chair and turned to Sulis.

"I dinna ken about what ye say."

And then the tinker widow turned to Amber and Dierdre.

"Ye are welcome tae stay as long as ye like. Ye hae been nought but helpful and kind tae me. Na everyone is like that in this world, and I truly appreciate ye."

Joanna sat down again, and Amber pressed her lips together to avoid laughing at Sulis, but only because that might have made things worse for Tomas.

Joanna hadn't really said anything about Sulis at all, but there was a general tittering in this area of the market. Apparently, all the widows nearby were amused by Sulis's having been subtly put down by Joanna.

Of course, Sulis couldn't just leave it well enough alone. She had to make a scene even bigger than the one she had already made. She had to have the last word. That was the kind of person she was.

Sulis stood up even taller and moved her head from side to side in a mocking way and raised her finger at Joanna and shook it at her as if she were a small child and not an elderly widow who deserved respect. When Sulis next spoke, it was as if she were making a speech to everyone in the whole town, it carried so well.

"Upon closer examination, the goods at this booth are na up tae my standards, and I will take my business and my ample money tae spend doon the way, where people are more respectful o their betters."

Sulis flounced off in what she plainly intended to be an imperious way.

But all the women in the area tittered again, putting the lie to the druidess's assumption that she had this whole town sewn up in the palm of her hand.

Naoi (9)

Amber helped Eileen walk all her children home that night, and the two of them had supper ready before Kelsey and Sasha got home. Amber could tell by the looks on their faces that they had been unsuccessful in their search for Lachlan the Dark. They nonetheless passed a pleasant evening playing with the children. The men were drilling at the castle and weren't present this evening but said they'd have dinner with the lasses the next night.

Sasha and Kelsey met Amber in her dreams briefly to reassure her that she would be touring the castle and the town.

The next morning, Tomas was there at the castle gate when Amber arrived. He was leaning listlessly against the fence, and he stayed that way even when she got there.

She stopped next to him and defiantly decided to look him in the eye — but with raised eyebrows.

"Good morning. I did na expect tae see ye here."

He didn't look at her, just kept staring at a hole in the road.

"Aye, I would na hae been, howsoever, Tavish just asked me tae escort ye aroond, right after Sulis left on one o her jaunts intae the forest."

Amber clapped a few times, ostensibly because she was happy to have him as a guide — but really to try and awaken Tomas from his stupor. It sort of worked.

He pushed off the fence with his elbow and — turning his back on her and leaving her to follow if she would — started walking through the gate into the castle courtyard.

She hurried to catch up, and walked by his side.

He walked through the castle courtyard and was opening a door to go inside when she grabbed his elbow to stop him. She knew the answer to the question she asked, but this wouldn't be any sort of tour if all he did was walk around and ignore her. She figured it was up to her to get them talking.

"What are those bins full o wood for?"

He slowly turned to look at them and then back at her.

"They're practice swords."

He tried to pull away and open the door again, but she held onto his elbow.

"Sae dae ye guards practice in this courtyard? When? I would like tae watch that."

He wrinkled his brow at her.

"The guards practice every afternoon, and sometimes intae the evening, like yesterday. But 'tis naught tae watch, just ordinary men keeping their skills braw sae they can dae their duty."

On a hunch, she pushed for more details, giving him a soft smile.

"Sae where and when dae the extraordinary men practice?"

Aha. He stood up a bit straighter at that. He did consider himself extraordinary. Unfortunately, in this context it meant he thought he was better than everyone else. He hadn't been like that before Sulis. If Amber ever got that woman alone when her powers were low, she would shove her face in the mud. What a B witch she was, corrupting someone as honorable as Tomas once had been.

He still was, she reminded herself. This wasn't really him, just a spell that Sulis had over him. And Amber needed to break him loose from it.

He was responding.

"We officers practice in a room Laird Malcomb designed for it, directly after breakfast."

She thought about it for moment.

"But that's now. Are ye missing practice on my account? Won't ye get in trouble?"

Until she'd mentioned trouble, he had been not quite smiling but at least not scowling. That changed. He sounded almost like a child, he was so cranky.

"Nay, I'm na gaun'ae get in trouble. I'm fifth in command o this whole place, Amber. All the men look up tae me, and Laird Malcomb and his nephew Alfred look tae me tae help them run things. I get a certain number o favors tae go along with that, and I spent one o those precious favors getting out o practice tae show ye aroond today. Least ye could dae is act appreciative o it instead o suggesting I'm gaun'ae get in trouble."

Before she could say anything else, he pushed through the door into the castle, once more leaving her to follow if she would.

She ran inside after him.

Not taking any notice whether she did or not, he stomped down the cold stone-on-stone hallway toward the corner, where there was another door.

Again she ran, so as not to allow him the satisfaction of losing her in the huge above-ground castle and thus shirking his duty as her escort for the day.

He looked resigned when she caught up to him at the door in the corner, and he sighed deeply before pushing it open and revealing a spiral staircase that went up into a tower. He started climbing up the stairs.

At least he wasn't running now, so it was easy for her to keep up. She could even talk while they climbed the stairs.

"Is this the tower where they kept that prisoner, Brian the Druid? Kelsey telt me aboot him."

He answered without looking back down the stairs at her.

"Aye. Howsoever, he was gone before I arrived. This is where they keep any prisoner. The underground palace is hardly a dungeon."

Amber knew better. She had seen dungeons in the underground palace — but her gut told her not to give this voodoo-doll version of Tomas any idea she knew better than him about what he considered his domain.

So she just slightly changed the subject.

"Is there a tower prison up at the top o each o the four corners o the above-ground castle, then?"

They had reached the top of the stairs now, and he proudly took out some keys and unlocked the prison room door, pushing it open so that she could see how small the turret room was.

"Nay. This corner faces the underground palace entrance and the cliffs that go doon tae land. No one would be able tae attack from that direction. The other three corners face the sea and land approaches. Those towers are reserved for archers when the need arises."

He had moved inside the room.

So she did also, surprised to see a bed in here. It really wasn't such a bad prison, albeit small.

"There are arrow-slit windows in this room, tae."

He moved over to one and looked out.

"Aye. There aren't always prisoners in here,

such as now. And anyway, the prisoner needs tae be able tae look oot and see what he's missing."

She looked out one of the windows for a moment.

"I see what ye mean. Let us move on. This room creeps upon me."

He nodded the slightest bit as he locked up the room and started down the stairs. Was he showing agreement?

They left the stairwell on the third floor of the castle, where he opened the doors to several apartments so that she could look inside, but they didn't go in. Each time, he would tell her whose apartment it was. He didn't use names, just said 'Laird Malcomb's eldest son and his family' or 'younger son and his family' or 'Laird Malcomb's elder nephew.'

At this last apartment, Amber got curious.

"After their wedding, will Eileen and her children move in here with Alfred?"

He nodded again.

"Aye. Even though Alfred's marrying a commoner and her bairns are common, Laird Malcomb and his wife — and especially his maw — are fond o them. Next, we can see the nursery where his maw takes care o them when they're here at the castle for feasts. I suppose she will always take care o them once they live here."

This made Amber smile, the thought of Eileen's lovely children being taken care of by someone here in the castle who was fond of them.

"Aye, I should like tae see that."

Was it her imagination, or was he walking more slowly now, even waiting for her to catch up with him if he did leave her behind?

They went back inside the stairwell and down a flight of stairs. But before they could leave on the second floor, a squadron of kilted soldiers with big swords strapped to their backs entered the stairwell through the same door they wished to exit, one at a time in single file.

The last man stopped and stared at Amber for a moment, then smiled and bowed his head slightly.

"Hello again, Amber. D'ye remember me? Cormac. We met on the cliffs the other day, and I saw ye at the feast the other night. I wonder if the next time there is a feast, ye might want tae—"

Tomas cut between the two of them.

"Get on yer way back tae yer squadron."

Cormac looked confused for a moment, and then he stood up straight and took the steps two at a time on his way up.

"Aye aye, Captain."

Shocked, Amber just stood there gazing at Tomas. He sure had broken out of his zombie stupor. His eyes looked a lot less glazed over, and his face was even flushed a bit.

He cleared his throat and opened the door for her, waiting for her to precede him through it.

"What? He canna be shirking his duty. We let a wee bit o that take hold, and there would be chaos."

Amber's natural inclination was to tease him,

but intuition told her that would be disastrous in his current state, so instead she simply smiled and went through the door he was holding into an older part of Laird Malcomb's above-ground castle, where the halls were wider and the stone building blocks darker.

She paused, unsure which door would lead into the nursery.

Tomas smiled slightly at her as he passed by. It was a friendly smile, and she almost didn't notice, it was so normal for him. Had been normal for him seven plus years ago, anyway.

He stopped at a set of double doors and opened them wide.

"Here we are, the nursery. There is na anyone here now."

Amber smiled as she went in.

"I can imagine Aodh and Niall playing in here, and little Deirdre supervising them."

Tomas went over to a hand carved rocking horse and stroked his hand over it.

"'Tis someaught of a spectacle, aye?"

Amber felt drawn to him then, as if some sort of tractor beam from his eyes had attached to her and was actively reeling her in. She went over and used the rocking horse as an excuse to get close, touching its sanded and painted smoothness with her own hands — and letting her shoulder nearly touch Tomas's shoulder.

"Mmmhmm, all that is in here is beautiful."

Their eyes met then, and his looked aware, but confused and unsure. His brow wrinkled then — in concentration, she thought — and he swallowed, making his Adam's apple go up and down pronouncedly before he spoke.

"Amber?"

Not breaking eye contact, she nodded at him slowly.

"Aye, 'tis me."

He reached for her. She knew that was what he was doing, reaching out to take her into an embrace that would heal the worry in both of them. It would feel like home, and she welcomed it with a triumphant smile. He was hers. They hadn't ever broken up. He'd simply disappeared from her life. He was hers, and she was going to reclaim him now with a wonderful warm embrace.

But as his hands slid over the rocking horse toward her, its smooth painted surface distracted him, and he looked down, away from her eyes. Once their eye contact was broken, his brow wrinkled in confusion once more, and he looked around the room as if seeing it for the first time.

And then he grabbed her hand and started walking briskly toward the double doors into the hallway.

"I hae tae get ye out o here."

He pushed through the double doors, then turned the opposite direction from where they'd come and hustled her down the dark stone hallway into another spiral stone stairwell. The door at the bottom opened out into a huge room with a bunch of plank wood counters and herbs hanging from the ceiling and a huge fireplace in the center. Amber gradually realized this was the castle kitchen. A bunch of women paused from kneading dough and cutting vegetables to look at them with surprised faces as Tomas hurried Amber through an open door and outside.

They were near the spot where she had first become aware of her surroundings when the song stopped making her want to jump off the cliff, which she could now see again.

He was walking her toward the stairway into the underground castle.

Her breath caught. Getting her out of here meant sending her home. She couldn't leave him, or he would fall right back under Sulis's spell again and she wouldn't be any closer to saving him then she had been when she first arrived.

But then she remembered that Tomas would need Tavish to send her home, and Tavish had agreed it was safer if they all stayed here in the past together. So she relaxed and just enjoyed being with Tomas. Enjoyed having his hand in hers once again.

Enjoyed it that is until they got to the bottom of the stairs and ran smack into Sulis.

Still in her white linen robes — now stained green and brown from the woods — the druidess grabbed Tomas away from Amber and whispered something in his ear.

Amber tried to get him away from her.

"Tomas, ye dinna hae tae go with her. Just tell her tae—"

But it was too late. As soon as Sulis whispered in his ear, Tomas's eyes clouded up again. His posture became listless — he became a zombie again.

Amber tried to talk to him, to snap him out of it.

"Tomas? Tomas!"

But Sulis was standing right there. Her close proximity to him must have made the spell stronger. He just stood there by his mistress's side, staring into space.

Not so with Sulis. She tossed her blonde hair back and then stood there regally with her pretty nose in the air, subtly but effectively snarling at Amber.

"Ye had yer try at getting him back, and ye failed. He wants me, na ye. Stay away from him, or I will see that ye dae, permanently."

Sulis went up the stairs as she said this, just about dragging Tomas behind her by the hand.

Amber followed them, even as they reached the top of the stairs and went walking toward the main castle entrance. Sulis's legs were longer than hers, though. She wouldn't be able to catch up without running after them, and that was far too undignified for what Amber had in mind.

Only slightly aware of the guards at the top of the stairs looking at her curiously, she called after Sulis.

"Ye better na harm him, or I will see that ye never harm anyone again — permanently."

The druidess merely threw up her other hand in a dramatic flair in response, just before she reached the castle gate and made Tomas open it for her. And then the two of them disappeared together into the great hall where the feast in

Sulis's honor had been the night before.

Amber's stomach growled.

The guard behind her snickered at that.

She turned around and looked at him. He was eating an apple.

"Are they serving the midday meal in the great hall nae?"

He nodded.

"Aye, howsoever, 'tis only for them as live in the castle, and the guards."

She gave him her most mischievous grin and glanced sideways at the kitchen door she and Tomas had come out of a few minutes before.

"Thank ye."

Before he had time to say you're welcome, she scrunched her nose at him and ran toward the kitchen door. She needed to break the spell Sulis had over Tomas. While he and Sulis were busy eating, maybe she could find something in Tomas's room that would help.

Deich (10)

Shocking the same women she had a few minutes ago when she and Tomas ran through the castle kitchen, Amber ran right through there again, not stopping when she got into the cold stone hallway but running all the way down to Tomas's pointy-topped bedroom door, opening it, and hastening to close it behind her.

She paused with her back against it. Breathing heavily. Expecting any moment to hear a castle resident ask what business she had in this room. And toss her out on her ear.

After a few minutes, she caught her breath. She was lucky today. She didn't hear anyone coming.

Nodding with pride in the instinct which had told her to run through the castle, thus giving people the least chance of seeing her, she turned to the room at hand.

Maybe Sulis had made some sort of voodoo doll of Tomas and hidden it here in this room, controlling him. Amber itched to find it — or anything that would help her break the spell.

First, she searched the chest of drawers. Five clean linen shirts, two clean kilts, two clean plaid overdresses, and five clean pairs of socks later, she moved on to the bed. It had been made, but she turned down the covers and searched between the blankets and even between the handmade mattress and the wooden platform it sat on before making the bed up again, having found nothing.

Finally, she lay down on the cold stone floor and looked under the bed. Ah, there were Tomas's weapons — his large claymore and his bow & quiver. She had drawn out the quiver and was searching among the arrows when she heard the door open.

Ready for a fight with Sulis, Amber got up with defiance in her eyes.

But it was Tomas. His glazed-over eyes traveled the room, then finally zeroed in on his quiver in her hand. The faintest hint of half a dozen different emotions passed over his face one by one in the next few moments: shock, unbelief, anger, fear, cunning — and was that last one … hope?

When he spoke, his voice was low and breathy, almost a whisper — like he was just as afraid as she was, of being overheard by people outside the room in the rest of the castle.

Like the two of them were in this together.

But his words were contrary.

"What are ye doing in here going through my stuff?" He pointed to the quiver. "Put that back where ye found it."

Not taking her eyes off his, she squatted and did as she was told. There hadn't been anything in the quiver but arrows, anyway. And then, seeing how this might be the last time she saw him, the last chance she got, she stood again and just laid it all out on the line for him. Quietly.

"I was trying tae find some aught that will get rid o this horrible influence she has ower ye, Tomas. Ye are na the same when she's aroond. Ye were weird and grumpy this morning, but the longer we bided together today, the more normal ye got. Ye were almost yer usual self — right afore she showed up. There has tae be some sort o... some aught she's using tae keep this hold on ye, and I was looking for it. I did na find it, though."

He stood still for a moment, and again she could almost see the wheels turning behind his eyes in his mind, processing what she had said. Even though his eyes were glazed over in that infernal zombiehood, she thought she detected the barest glimpses of a dozen emotions running through his eyes quickly, like the spinning wheels of a mechanical slot machine.

Unfortunately, this time they landed on anger.

He leaned into her face and pointed at the door. At odds with his angry mood, however, he still kept his voice down.

"I was ready tae just accept that ye were a nosy person in here poking intae my business as some-aught o an auld friend. I was gaun'ae just let ye go and na think any more o it — excepting tae say dinna dae it again. But now ye hae gone and dragged Sulis intae this. Ye shouldna be badmouthing her. 'Tis unattractive. It makes me want tae tell ye tae leave and never come back."

Amber growled the tiniest bit.

In an attempt to let off the steam his little speech had built up inside her, she stomped her feet and brought her arms down with force to her sides.

"I shouldna be badmouthing Sulis? Tomas, that woman tried tae make me jump off a cliff! She has ye doing a job ye are na fit tae do, just tae satisfy her drive for material things. She has ye fighting with yer brother, whom I know ye love more than ye could ever love a woman ye hae only known a few months. That woman is evil, Tomas, evil and conniving and ruthless! And she's manipulating ye. Canna ye see that?"

Oh, it was on, now.

He got in her face.

His own face looked angry, but his body was still slumped and zombielike. His hand that had been pointing to the door dropped to his side. Contrary to his posture, his voice came out like an angry hiss, and he lapsed into English.

"She didn't make you go to that cliff, Amber. Do you know how stupid that sounds? She is not manipulating me. She's my girlfriend, and I'm with her now. We've been together three months."

Amber put her hands on her hips and stood up straight. His zombified brain was denying reality, but his body seemed to remember her. Maybe if she appealed to his body, his brain would snap out of it. And if it did, then heck with this long-time-ago place.

Once Tomas snapped out of his zombie coma, she was going to go find Tavish and have him take them back to their time. She would get Tomas on a plane far away from here. Just keep running and never let Sulis near him again — or take him to his parents' faire. They would help her protect him.

She didn't dare touch him yet, though. She needed to soften him up a little more, like she had this morning. Gazing into his eyes with all the emotion she felt — all the love bottled up inside her — she lapsed into English as well and made her voice as soft and loving as she could, considering her frustration.

"Tomas, I care about you, or I would've gone home as soon as I saw..."

No, don't continue along those lines. Better not to mention the B witch. She tried again.

"Don't you remember half an hour ago, Tomas? When you and I were talking like old times? You showed me around the castle and we both really liked the rocking horse in the nursery?"

His face bunched up in grumpiness like when they had met out in front of the castle this morning, and one side of his mouth rose in an ironic smile, as if what she said couldn't possibly be true.

But his body turned away from the door and toward her.

And his eyes stayed on her. They weren't nearly as glazed over as they had been this morning. Was she imagining it, was there a glimmer of recognition in them?

He evaded her question, but when he spoke, he didn't sound angry anymore, just determined.

"I don't know what you're doing here, Amber, but in this time, do you realize how dangerous it is to barge into a man's room uninvited? This castle is a fortress full of guards who mean business and train with swords every day to keep in shape for fending off the Raiders — who are other Scots. These people fight against each other all the time. This isn't some game. This is a real castle and there are real guards outside and they have real weapons, Amber."

The earnestness in his voice was at such odds with the way his body stood limp that for a moment she was at a loss for what to say. But she decided it was good that he was still talking to her, and that she should encourage him to keep on doing so.

Almost like he was programmed, he seemed to shy away from some subjects, while other subjects were fine. She guessed at which subjects might be fine.

"But I should be safe now that you're here. I mean, you're the captain of the guards, so they'll do as you say."

He stood stock still again, and then he nodded the tiniest little bit, while at the same time moving closer to her so that they were standing side by side, both facing the door. What he said didn't make sense at first.

"Yes, I am the captain of the guards who work in the underground castle. They do as I say most of the time, but there have been times when I didn't feel like I was in charge."

He sounded so puzzled and confused and lost. She longed to hug him and tell him he didn't need to be in charge of these guards, that the two of them would go back to the future and have a life together with nothing to do with all this. He had the business aspects of the Renaissance Fairee to run, and when he was himself, he was really keen on running them.

Soon.

Soon she would be able to hold him and say these things. He was coming out of the funk, just as he had this morning. Each moment, he was less zombified and more like the Tomas she knew and loved.

She just had to keep him talking a while longer.

"Well it makes sense that they wouldn't completely think of you as their captain. I mean, you've only been here a week, but the other captain — Alfred is it?"

He nodded once.

She shrugged and gave him a sympathetic smile.

"Well, Alfred is someone they've known their whole lives, so of course they're going to follow his orders more readily than they follow those of a relative stranger—"

His body was stock still and slumped, but his head was shaking 'no,' vigorously— and then he touched the back of her hand, and she stopped speaking out of shock more than anything. His touch felt so wonderful, like coming home after a hard day at work to a surprise party with all your favorite friends and family — and a homemade cake. A simple touch from him sent that kind of warmth through her.

With a mind of its own, her hand turned to hold his, palm to palm, and they stood there like that quietly for several moments. She was dying to ask him if this meant they were getting back together, but something weird was going on. The real Tomas seemed to have control of his body, the Tomas who was going home to see to the business side of the faire.

But his speech and his thoughts? Amber hadn't snapped those away from the zombie Sulis had recreated inside Tomas's head half an hour ago, undoing all the progress Amber had made this morning. Not just yet. Amber would have to give it a little while. But in the meantime, holding hands with him was comforting.

But he had interrupted her for a reason, and soon he spoke again, his face so confused it made her heart ache.

"It isn't because I'm not Alfred. That's not why they sometimes don't listen to me. They do it to him too. We've talked about it. We don't really know what it is, but something's going on. I think it has to do with that Lachlan the Dark. Tavish and I have a plan to catch the man, and then we'll question him and find out."

A pang of guilt hit Amber, for keeping the secret of Sasha's wedding vision from Tomas. Still holding his hand, she longed to sit down with him on the bed and get comfortable, but it seemed like anything that hinted at being more than friends set off some sort of trigger that brought back Sulis's zombie full force. Amber had to keep reminding herself that it had taken a couple hours to bring him out of the zombie state this morning.

And it had taken Sulis just one whisper in his ear to put him right back there.

But where was the B witch now?

Ha. Apparently, it had taken Sulis so much magic to zombify Tomas again that she was back out in the woods now, sinking her teeth into trees. Or whatever she did to soak up more of that druid magic.

Amber gently squeezed Tomas's hand.

"You're probably right. It probably does have something to do with Lachlan. You'll fix that soon. I know you will."

There was a lull in their conversation then. Still clinging to his hand, Amber fished around in her mind for another innocuous thing to talk about. But maybe it was better if they didn't talk. Maybe now was the time to see if her body could bring his out of the stupor. As friends, so that she didn't set off the zombie alarm.

She looked up into his eyes.

They were doing that slot machine thing again.

Better make her move before they settled on any one emotion. She slowly moved in for a hug, raising her arms up over his shoulders so that she could clasp them around the back of his neck. This was going to work, she could feel it in her bones. Especially once they were hugging.

Ah. Peace at last.

Settling down for a deep rest in his embrace, she laid her head against his chest and held him close. They stood there for the longest time, and it was heaven when his arms moved around her waist to hug her too. They started to rock back and forth slowly, slow dancing with no music.

She had him back. Tears came to her eyes, and then whispered into his ear the question that had been on her mind for seven years.

"What happened on your eighteenth birthday, Tomas? Why did you disappear out of my life?

He trembled as soon as she started whispering.

Elation went through her body, making her tingle all over. She clung to him in return and spoke the thoughts of her heart.

"Can we get back together again?"

But he was no longer returning her embrace.

And he didn't answer, just stumbled away from her and hurried out the door.

Aon Deug (11)

Tomas had to find Sulis. If he didn't go look for her right this minute, something horrible would happen. It could not be allowed to happen. He had to find Sulis. Right now. Or he would be sorry.

What would happen, anyway?

Pain shot into his head from his eyes.

He had to find Sulis...

She wasn't in the great hall anymore.

How about if he asked this man—

As soon as he had that thought, he heard her Southern accent in his head.

"Tomas honey, in these times you cannot let anyone think you don't know where everything is and where you need to be."

He had to find Sulis by himself.

He went toward the stairway down into the underground palace. She was often down there. It was sort of a long way though. And he had to find her soon, her terrible consequences would ensue. Better hurry.

But as soon as he thought of running, he heard her words again.

"Tomas honey, you know you really must set a stately example for the men under your command."

Walking, it was.

And all the while he looked for her, the story his dad had told him and Tavish on their eighteenth birthday played over and over again in Tomas's mind.

~*~

Oor ancestor Sean MacGregor was between a rock and a hard place. You see, Sean liked gambling. It didna matter what he gambled on. Oh sure, he would play games o dice, but even the little things in life were subject tae gambling for him. How soon were the lambs gaun'ae come? How soon was the snow gaun'ae fall? How many kittens would be in the next litter?

The will tae gamble put Sean intae a fever, it did. And as is always the case with men who hae a weakness such as gambling, there were those who took advantage o him. They baited him tae gamble, knowing he couldna always win and that they would hae his money.

Because o his gambling, Sean owed more money than he would ever make in his lifetime, and no one would give him loans anymore.

Now Sean had three sons and two daughters tae feed, as wull as his wife and his maw and his wife's maw. The clan would help, aye, but as all MacGregors are, he was a proud man who didna want the charity o others.

One gloomy Scottish day on the moor, Sean was out gathering peat for the family fire. He had gone farther than he normally would, because 'twas an exceptionally cauld winter, and all the fuel nearby had already been burned. He was all by himself, and verra far out o earshot from anyone he knew.

He was getting close tae the mountain when he noticed there were some wee lights up there. With naught left tae lose, he slung his large sack with a few clumps o peat ower his shoulder and climbed up tae see what they were.

When he got close enough for his eyes tae show him the goings-on, he could na believe them. A large hole had been dug intae the side o the mountain, and men were going in with picks and coming out with chunks o gauld.

He knew 'twas gauld, for he had seen raw nuggets in their dirt-covered form afore. Ye see, back in those days, they used tae trade in nuggets o gauld, na sae much in coins as we dae now.

Sean felt the drool dribbling doon his chin and doon his neck as he watched the men come oot with all this wealth while he hid in the brush and heather. Why should those men hae all that gauld? He could go in and dig some oot for himself. That would solve all o his problems, said the devil on Sean's left shoulder.

The angel on his right shoulder argued that he wasna likely tae go home with nary being tarnished by the experience.

Sean sat there quite a while, stroking his beard and thinking this through afore he ran ower and fell in line with the men going in with their picks.

Only he didna hae a pick.

Just when Sean had this thought, a man stepped oot from between two boulders and held oot a pick tae Sean. The man was auld, and he wore a long white robe o a cut Sean had never seen afore. 'Twas made o the brawest white linen, with patterns embroidered intae the collar. Only 'twas stained green and brown from life in the wild.

"Here," said this grizzled auld one, holding oot the pick tae Sean.

Sean wasna one tae look a gift horse in the mouth, sae he took the pick and was on his way, na even pausing when he called ower his shoulder, "Thank ye."

Sean fell back in line with the men just as they entered the cave. 'Twas dank and dark, but Sean could almost smell the gauld up ahead, sae he didna mind.

Digging oot the gauld took longer than Sean thought it would — all day and all night for three days, just tae dig oot enough that he thought he could repay his debts. Food would coome in, and the men would lie doon on the grass tae sleep, but otherwise, they were digging and picking and pounding tae get oot the gauld.

And Sean thought tae himself, "Why should I stop with just enough gauld tae repay my debts? Let me work another three days, and I shall have enough to last the rest o my life, and even be able tae gamble some o it."

Sae Sean dug and ate and slept and dug some moore for another three days and three nights, until he had na only enough gauld tae repay all o his debts, but enough tae set himself up comfortable fer life and still hae some for gambling.

When he had all o this, he hoarded it up intae his sporran and his other pouches and made his way oot with some men who are heading oot, picks ower their shoulders.

Howsoever, when Sean got out o the cave, who should be lingering there but the auld man who had given him the pick?

At foremaist, Sean thought the auld man only wanted his pick back, for his hand was oot as if waiting for it. This Sean gladly gave him.

But the pick wasna what the auld man was after. His beady eyes studied Sean with a malevolent intelligence, and his voice came oot harsh next he spake.

"Let us hae what ye got oot o the cave, aye?"

Now, giving the man back the gauld that Sean had worked sae hard for six days and six nights tae get was the last thing on his mind. Nay, he was looking aboot for some aught tae use as a weapon in order tae beat the man doon sae that he could flee with the gauld.

Not all o oor ancestors were honest, sorry tae say.

While Sean was thinking this, the auld man called out tae several men aroond him, who came ower and seized Sean and tied him up. Once he was helpless, the auld man's beady eyes were on him again.

"Well nae," says he. "I can take the gauld by force, ye ken. Howsoever, 'tis curious I am, what ye will give me for it."

Sean opened his mouth tae suggest what he might give.

But the auld man gestured, and his cronies gagged Sean as wull as they had tied him up.

Sean couldna speak if his life depended on it, and fair tae likely it did.

The auld man was speaking, puffing on a pipe he had lit while Sean was being gagged.

"I will tell ye what ye will give me in exchange for the gauld. It willna be all bad, ye ken. I will get rid o this reckless abandon ye hae at gambling yer wages away — and then some. Sae ye hae that gift as wull as the gauld tae pay back what ye hae squandered. In fact, I will dae this now. Tae show my good faith."

Sean felt his mind scramble when the auld man put his hand on Sean's forehead. Visions o all the wages he'd held and lost went spinning aroond in his mind, followed by a whirlpool that spun aroond faster and faster till it drained out the bottom o his nose in a bunch o snot that he blew intae his sleeve.

"There nae," said the auld man. "Yer urge tae gamble is gone forever. Nay need tae thank me, for now yer debt is greater than afore, when all ye did was steal my gauld."

Sean fought against his bindings and his gag, thinking, "Where did the auld man get the idea this all was his gauld?" Ye see, this was Sean's clan's territory — oor territory. Sae the gauld was rightfully the clan's, didna the auld man ken?

Sean could hae sworn up and doon he hadna said a word o these thoughts.

Even so, the auld man threw back his head and laughed. "The land doesna belong tae yer clan. Nay one owns the land. 'Tis older than all the rest o us put together. Nay, the land isna owned. And what is in the land isna owned either, till it is brought oot with the work o one's hands." He looked askance at the men who obeyed his every word. "Or the hands o those one owns."

Hearing the auld man say that he owned these other men greatly disturbed Sean — as ye can wull imagine. On hearing this, he looked intae the eyes o the men who had bound him.

They were glazed ower, na quite clear. But there was nay sign o fear in these men. They were resigned tae their lot. They didna look at all unhappy... just na sae delighted as they might hae been tae be digging up gauld.

The auld man brought his beady eyes right up in front o Sean's.

"Aye, they are na unhappy. And what I hae in mind for ye, 'tis na sae bad even as they hae it.

Ye wouldna need tae serve me and my line yerself. Only the fourth son born tae ye would need tae — and every fourth son barn intae yer line after that — and only once they've reached the age o five and twenty. Only tell me ye agree tae that, and I will tell my men tae let ye go with yer gauld back tae yer clan and live yer happy life."

Now Sean was still trussed up, and he couldna give his aye or nay till they removed the gag from his mouth. He took the opportunity tae think the offer ower.

On the one hand, there was slavery for his fourth born son — who had na in fact been born yet, and might never be — and neither had the fourth born sons o any in his line. That last bit was verra distant for him, ye ken. On the other hand, he was already trussed up, sae these men would hae little difficulty at all in beating him senseless and taking the gauld from him.

He nodded tae show he was ready tae give his answer.

The auld man cackled in a frightening though somehow still humorous way and gestured that the men should undo Sean's gag, which they did — still leaving the trusses.

Sean took a deep breath in order tae give out the speech he had prepared in his moments o contemplation.

But the white-robed auld man interrupted him.

"We will na hae a speech. Just tell me aye or nay. Will ye be gang home with enough gauld tae pay off yer debts — and then some, I daresay — or nay?"

It seemed tae Sean that even the glassy eyed slaves o the auld man leaned forward tae hear his answer. There really wasna a choice, howsoever.

"Aye."

The auld man leaned forward and put his hand tae his ear.

"What's that?"

Sean spoke up loudly.

"Aye."

The auld man turned aroond and looked smugly at all o his servants, nodding mostly tae himself.

"Ye all are witness tae that. He took this on willingly, ye ken?"

They all nodded, and then the auld man gestured, and one o them took off Sean's right boot.

Sean looked at him quizzically.

The auld man hollered, and yet another man came running up the hill from doon below wth some aught glowing in his hand. Sean couldn't make out what 'twas for the longest time, but then he gasped.

Soon as he did, the men ganged up and forced the gag back in his mouth and then held doon his body by sitting on it all ower, leaving his right ankle exposed.

Sean tried tae scream when the brand hit his ankle, but he couldna get wind with all the men sitting on him, let alone get the wind oot o him with the gag in his mouth.

And then the auld man touched the branded place, and the pain disappeared — but in its place came the oddest sensation through his whole body. Visions o all his descendants flashed afore his eyes, and each fourth born son was born with this mark aroond his right ankle.

In the vision, Sean saw that the mark was a ring o standing stones.

~*~

After the story, they had all looked at the standing stones birthmark which Tavish clearly had on his right ankle. It had been so disturbing at the time, and sometimes, like now, Tomas thought of Sulis's white robes and compared them to the robes in the story. His mind was going a million miles an hour with fear and worry and even guilt.

But then he found Sulis. He didn't even know what she whispered in his ear, only that all the turmoil in his mind went away.

Dà Dheug (12)

Beset by a sudden drench of tears and choking sobs, Amber ran out of the castle and through the town to the weaver shop, where she flung herself on the floor in front of Eileen's spinning wheel, laid her head in the woman's lap, and wept.

Eileen stopped working and stroked Amber's hair.

"Ye must get hold of yerself." She projected her voice across the room to her children. "Gae on ootside and play, ye bairns." She waited a minute while they complied, then spoke in the same soothing voice as before. "What is it?"

Amber was sobbing so hard, she could barely

breathe, let alone talk.

"I... He... Sulis..."

Eileen handed her a handkerchief.

"Here ye are. Try yer best tae pull yerself together now."

Amber gratefully blew her nose. Doing so helped her gain her composure a bit, so she got up and sat on her stool and began carding wool after she wiped her tears as well, taking several deep breaths in order to calm her breathing and stop the choking effect.

"I thank ye. Oh, 'tis Tomas. Ye wouldna ken from how he behaves now, but he is a good man, Eileen. A good man who is trapped under Sulis's thumb."

Eileen watched Amber card for a moment, as if she expected her to break down again, but when she didn't, Eileen went back to spinning the wool into yarn.

"'Twould na be the first time a pretty lass brought a good man doon. Nay, 'twould na."

Thankful for the affirmation, Amber gave Eileen a grateful look.

"I did spend the day with him yesterday, ye ken. At first, he was grumbling, but toward the end o it he seemed wull. Howsoever, then she showed up and whispered in his ear — and he transformed once again tae this zombie—"

Eileen put a hand on Amber's elbow.

"Pray tell, what be a zombie?"

Amber cast about the room for an answer that would be suitable.

"'Tis a creature in a story I heard once. A

mindless slave."

Eileen nodded.

"'Tis a suitable name for him, aye."

Eileen studied Amber's face a moment, appearing to be making a decision. And then she lowered her voice to barely a whisper, darting glances over at the male weavers at their looms across the room.

"There is a good enchantress nearby tae the south. Elsbeth may be able tae help him. Mayhap she is powerful enough tae break the spell. Howsoever, ye mustna go alone. 'Tis tae dangerous. Seumas knows the way — everyone roond here does — and if ye ask him tae go with ye — and perhaps Tavish as wull — I'm certain they will."

Amber wiped the last of her tears away with a small smile for Eileen, then held up the handkerchief with a questioning look in her eyes.

Smirking, Eileen pointed to the wash buckets on the other side of the looms.

Amber put the handkerchief in with the white clothes and then helped Eileen spin some more.

But the first chance she got, she excused herself to go to the privy, asked someone how to get to Elsbeth's, and set off on her own to the south.

~*~

Amber expected the woods to be scary, going by Eileen's warning. So she was pleasantly surprised that the birds were singing and even the sun was shining and the flowers blooming as she made her way to the witch's little cottage by a stream, deep in the woods.

Only two things kept it from being a pleasant stroll.

One, she had the uneasy feeling someone was following her.

Every once in a while she would pause at what she thought a random point and whip her head around in the direction she thought she felt the pursuit from. But she didn't see anything. She thought she heard something a few times, but with all the birds singing, it was hard to be sure.

Two, she was going to visit a witch.

Three days ago, Amber would've laughed if you told her someone was a witch. She hadn't believed in such things. But with the evidence that magic actually did exist all around her because of this trip into the past, a healthy amount of fear loomed in her mind. Would she herself fall into some sort of spell as soon as she saw the woman?

But when she got there, she laughed.

The enchantress's cottage was adorable. Different-colored river rocks piled up on top of each other to make walls. The roof was made from a million handfuls of straw. Amber walked up the stone pathway through the grass and flowers and knocked on the cute little maple-wood door.

"Aye, be with ye in a moment," called out a sweet woman's voice from within.

While she waited, Amber took stock of the cottage. There was smoke coming out of the little stone chimney, and little maple-wood shutters covered the tiny windows. The whole cottage could fit in her parents' living room. She wanted one just like it.

The little door opened, and inside was a woman as pretty as Eileen, only thirty years older. Her smile was tentative, but welcoming.

"Hello, I suspect ye know I'm Elsbeth."

Amber found herself stumbling over her words, the woman had such a presence.

"Aye. Eileen told me o ye. She says ye might be able tae help me — or rather, tae help my friend Tomas. I'm Amber."

After briefly looking over Amber's shoulder for a moment for some strange reason perhaps only a witch would understand, Elsbeth stepped to the side and opened the door wider.

"Come in."

The cottage looked cozy from outside the door, with a fire in the grate of the little stone fireplace and a handwoven rag rug on the hardwood floor.

But something in her gut made Amber hesitate. The decision to cross the threshold of this house seemed monumental. But she'd walked all the way out here just to see this woman, so it would be silly to turn around and walk all the way back without even talking to her.

Amber went in and paused, looking about while her eyes adjusted to the firelight.

There were drawings of people mounted on the wattle and daub that sealed the river rock walls, and the only furnishings were a bed, two chairs, and a tiny kitchen table.

But the fourth wall grabbed Amber's attention, once she could see. It was full of little cubbyholes that held the most random collection of things: feathers, tiny little sticks of different varieties, stones, mushrooms, whole leaves, tiny glass jars with different colored liquids...

Elsbeth gestured to one of the chairs and sat down on the other side of the tiny table.

"Sae Amber, I will save ye the trouble o making small talk and just ask ye now — why hae ye come tae see me?"

Amber searched Elsbeth's eyes for any sign of mocking, but they looked sweet and kind. She decided she was going to trust Elsbeth. After all, Tavish and Kelsey trusted Eileen, and Eileen had said Elsbeth was a good enchantress.

"'Tis a long story."

Elsbeth rested her head in her hands, which she had propped on the table by her elbows.

"I hae naught tae do all the day. Dae tell."

Somehow, looking at the witch was tiring. So while she talked, Amber slouched in her chair and studied the slats of the ceiling that held up the straw of the roof. She had to concentrate in order to pick out only the details in her story which would make sense to a woman of this time.

"When I was fourteen, my parents finally let me volunteer at the Ren... at the market fair for the summer. 'Twas far enough away from oor haime that I had tae camp there overnight two days a week. I'd never stayed away from haime afore, and it gave me a lot o freedom. I met Tomas there, and we had sae much in common.

152

We were inseparable whenever I was at the fair.
I fell in love with Tomas, and I am certain he fell
in love with me tae. For four summers this went
on. I thought we would be together forever —
that once we were grown, we would be marrit.
But the day after his eighteenth birthday, Tomas
disappeared from my life. Went away withoot
saying where. All his kin went, tae."

Elsbeth's face looked sorry for her to the
extent Amber hadn't expected. It was almost as
if Elsbeth were living through what Amber
described, the sorrow in the enchantress's eyes
was that deep.

"Such a loss is hard to bear. It strengthens us,
but the pain... Most believe the pain is not worth
the gain in strength of character."

What an odd thing to say.

Amber had to think about it for a minute
before she even realized what it meant. Deciding
she had been paid a complement — albeit a
weird one — she smiled the tiniest bit and gave
the enchantress a little nod before continuing her
tale.

"That happened seven years ago. I tried tae
forget him, tae fall in love and marry anoother,
but 'twas a losing cause. I despaired o ever being
marrit."

Elsbeth closed her eyes and wrinkled her
forehead, as if she were experiencing the despair
that Amber had gone through.

It freaked Amber out a little. Before going on
with her story, she waited patiently for Elsbeth to
relax and slough off the despair and open her

eyes to listen again.

"But seven days ago, a mutual friend called me — invited me here tae come work with her and Tomas's twin brother Tavish. I came right away, sure that Tomas would be here tae."

Elsbeth was smiling now, and it looked just like she was hopeful that she would see Tomas once she arrived at Kelsey's worksite.

Amber shook her head a little, to clear her mind of such a fanciful idea.

"Wull, Tomas is here all right, but with his … intended, Sulis."

Elsbeth's shoulders slumped.

Forgetting for a moment how strange this was, to have the woman living through the emotions Amber had, she gave her a sympathetic nod before she realized how silly that looked and put on a serious face, appealing to Elsbeth for whatever power she had to change the situation.

"This lass Sulis isna normal, Elsbeth. She has him under a spell o some sort. He isna himself when he's aroond her. His eyes glaze ower and his body is unanimated. He's what we call a zombie where we come from: a mindless slave. Howsoever, Sulis goes intae the woods often. Kelsey says it's tae renew her powers, that a whole lot o her magic is used up keeping the spell on Tomas. Mayhap ye would understand that?"

Elsbeth shook her head no the tiniest bit.

"I ken the druids. Doesna everyone? But nay, I am na one o them. If it please ye, go on with the tale."

Amber sighed, then continued.

"Wull, when Sulis is gone off tae the woods tae soak in their sap or some aught—"

Elsbeth laughed at Amber's joke, and Amber gave her a small smile.

"When she goes off into the woods and I can be aroond Tomas by oorselves, he comes out o his daze. It takes a few hours, but he does return just about tae normal. But as soon as she returns — and she whispers in his ear, I hae noticed — then he's a zombie again. Elsbeth, ye hae tae help me break the spell of hopeless zombie-ism she has ower him. Please say ye will."

But Elsbeth's welcoming smile was now a resigned smile, and as she spoke, she slowly got up and showed Amber to the door of her tiny cottage.

"I canna help ye. Only true love can break the curse o false love. If there is one who Tomas truly loves, then his love for her can overcome this curse. 'Tis the only thing which can."

Amber's heart sank.

Once upon a time, Tomas had loved her, but he sure didn't today. If only it were her love for him that mattered, she felt sure that she could save him from a life of servitude. How would they ever rescue him from Sulis now?

Still, none of this was Elsbeth's fault. The woman had been nothing but kind and sympathetic. So Amber gave the enchantress the most grateful smile she could manage.

"Wull, thank ye for yer time."

Elsbeth said a farewell before closing the door

softly.

"Ye were well tae come."

Amber slumped as she was left to look at the charming little maplewood door. What a disappointment.

However, all thoughts of Tomas's plight fled Amber's mind as soon as she turned around. The forest, once warm, was now getting dark, and it was shadowy and spooky. An owl hooted nearby, making her jump up a foot as she swiftly walked through the creepy trees.

She was hitting her stride when something came at her from the shadows. Scooping up her long plaid skirts, she broke into a run. But she couldn't see the ground very well with all that fabric in her arms.

A tree root got in her way, and she tripped and fell hard.

And then the eerie laughter of the man who had tried to run her off the cliffs back in her own time came toward her swiftly. The laughter of Lachlan the Dark.

Trì Deug (13)

Pushing herself up off the damp leafy forest floor, Amber willed herself to be angry instead of afraid. Looking around for a branch that she could use as a weapon, she took a deep breath so that there would be force behind her voice when she spoke, instead of it coming out as a squeak from her fear-constricted throat. She spotted a good branch and grabbed it. She used English, since there was no one else around and no need to put on her Gaelic and try to fit in.

"Why are you following me, Lachlan?"

She couldn't see him, but she turned around when his voice gave away his location.

"The better to catch you with, my dear."

The menace in his voice made the hair on her neck stand up, but she was not going to cower in fear. Her self-defense coach had told her that was what predators wanted, so in all cases she should go down fighting, even if it was just biting and scratching. He had also told her to scream bloody murder, but that was hardly going to do any good out here in the middle of the forest. She was far enough away from Elsbeth's now to be out of earshot.

She felt strongest when she was being snarky, so she poured it on.

"Very funny. You're hardly a wolf, though. More like an uppity little puppy."

A twig snapped, giving away his new location and making her turn again. He was getting closer, but he was moving very slowly and circling around, trying to be stealthy.

Yeah, stealthy.

She had barely any warning when he launched himself at her, only the movement of some branches at the corner of her eye to the left. Determined to go down fighting, she raised the branch up to defend herself.

But before Lachan could touch her, Tomas swept in again. He shoved the other man so hard, the man's head hit a tree and he slumped down onto the ground.

Amber opened her mouth to ask Tomas what he was doing here, but before she could, he turned around and leaned down, motioning for her to get on his back.

"I don't know how long he'll be out," Tomas said, "but I want to get you as far away from here as possible while he is."

Seeing the sense in that – and feeling so much relief she almost collapsed — she did as he asked, thankful that the long skirts of the day were full enough to allow it.

He started running as soon as she had locked her ankles around the front of him and grabbed his shoulders. She'd ridden on his back like this many times during a game they used to play at the faire, and this brought it all back to her as the trees went whooshing by. More owls hooted, but they were just lending atmosphere to an adventure she was having with her favorite person in the world.

And it was so nice, being close to him like this. Breathing in the warm woodsy scent of him. Feeling his muscles tense and his heart beating. Her body wanted to hug him close while she clung to him, to put her head against his shoulder and soak in the closeness of him...

And why shouldn't she?

The woman who claimed him did so under false pretenses. She didn't love him, and he didn't love her. It was just her artifice that kept him following her around like a lost puppy.

He'd been Amber's for four whole years, and he'd never broken up with her, just disappeared. And they'd been so good together. Even now, riding on his back, she already felt like she'd come home.

But she didn't dare say so.

She didn't dare mention any of these thoughts to him.

When it came to love between a man and woman, the language of the body was a lot more reliable than the language people spoke – so long as you didn't bring lust into it too soon. She'd made that mistake a few times and lived to regret it.

Talking would have been awkward anyway. Nothing she wanted to say was appropriate for his supposed social situation as the cherished intended of the B witch. Blech. Amber threw up a little in her mouth just thinking about what that woman really intended to do with Tomas according to Kelsey: leave him here as her slave in order to supervise his other slaves and loot the underground castle before Kelsey's client Mr. Blair ever came to possess it.

That was no kind of life for Tomas! He was bright and competent. He deserved to do as he wished and go home to manage his parents' business at the Renaissance Fairee. That was his real life. All this was just playing pretend. No, worse, it was a trap the B witch had snared him in.

So the whole time Tomas was running with her on his back toward Laird Malcomb's castle, Amber did just what she wanted to. She hugged him and put her head against his shoulder and soaked in the nearness of him without saying a word. She caressed his back and kissed his neck and gave him all the love she had despaired of ever giving him.

She might've squeezed him with her legs, too. She wasn't sure.

And then they got back to his room in the castle.

When he put her down, the separation was almost unbearable for her.

But he spoke as if unaffected.

"We need to wait for Tavish and Kelsey and their friends Sasha and Seumas. They're chasing Lachlan, and hopefully they'll find him while he's knocked out. I was with them, trying to help, but then I needed to get you to safety."

What a roller coaster ride. She'd been riding high only a moment ago, and now she was crashing down. He didn't seem at all affected by her closeness, the way she was by his. He must've moved on to someone else even before he met the B witch. He...

She did a double take on Tomas.

His eyes were clear, and he was talking sense. He wasn't a zombie at all right now. And the only person he was with was her. She was affecting him, even if he didn't acknowledge it. Maybe he did have feelings for her, but he didn't want to admit it. What had Elsbeth said? Did he have to show his feelings, or admit them?

She narrowed her eyes at him.

"Why were you so intent on rescuing me, then? If catching Lachlan was the bigger priority, why didn't you do that instead of grabbing me and taking me here?"

He looked down and away, fussing with the hair on the back of his head.

"Everybody knows women and children come first in a rescue situation."

He was in denial! His body language screamed it: avoiding her gaze and fidgeting with something else.

The spark of hope that had bloomed in her when Kelsey called, the hope she had nurtured during her journey to Scotland — and that she thought had died when she realized Sulis was Tomas's girlfriend — that spark of hope bloomed again in Amber's heart.

But she didn't dare touch him right now.

Call it feminine intuition, but somehow she just knew she had to let him make every first move.

Even though she had just ridden on his back in a very intimate way for the past half hour, she knew beyond a shadow of a doubt that she didn't dare reach out and touch him now, or he would withdraw, and she might never have a chance to try and get him to admit his feelings for her.

Instead, she needled him with her words. This wasn't unusual. She'd always teased him.

"But you'd already rescued me when you knocked him out. He was right there, incapacitated. You could've just as easily grabbed him and brought him here as me, and then you could have locked him up in the dungeons everyone says are downstairs, when we know full well they're ancient palace rooms, not dungeons."

He went from playing with the hair on the back of his head to sitting down on the bed and playing with the bedspread, and then quickly got up off the bed. Was that the hint of a blush she saw on his face?

Unfortunately, before she could get an answer out of him, everyone else came in the room.

Amber made a sour face at Kelsey. She couldn't help it. Here she and Tomas were — so close, and yet so far — and in come two happy couples, hands casually resting on each other.

Tomas, on the other hand, brightened up. Was he relieved to not be alone with her anymore?

"Did you get him?"

Tavish looked at Amber for a moment as if she might have developed a wasting sickness while he was away and he was checking to see if she still lived.

"No, and it's much worse."

Tomas's brow wrinkled.

"How it could be any worse?"

Kelsey came over and hugged Amber.

"Lachlan's after Amber. Specifically. He had plenty of opportunities to take other people easily, and he ignored them to follow her. He's been following her ever since she got here — and even before she came here, remember? We don't know why, but it doesn't matter. All that matters is keeping Amber safe. And the best way to do that is to catch him and keep him locked up."

Tomas briefly looked around at everyone else's faces, but when he saw that they were all nodding in agreement with Kelsey's assertion that Amber was the target, he flew into full-on protection mode, stuffing the arrow-slit windows with extra blankets — presumably to block the sound of their voices from getting to anyone outside. The castle walls were certainly thick enough to prevent it otherwise.

"Okay, that's it. Amber, don't go to Eileen's anymore to sleep. You're staying here with me—"

"But you share this room with Sulis —"

He made a dismissive gesture — dismissive of the woman he usually followed around like a dog on a leash.

"Sulis left this morning on some overnight errand, something about not being able to function with walls around her. So it's fine, and until we catch Lachlan — which we will, soon — Amber's going to stay in here. It's the safest place, a virtual stronghold. He won't be able to get in here. Seumas, tell the guards to be on the lookout for him."

The redheaded highlander nodded, kissed his redheaded woman — Sasha — and ducked out of the room.

Tomas went under the bed for his sword and his bow and arrows, then turned toward Amber.

"Stay in this room. There's a chamber pot over there in the corner, and I'll have someone bring you something to eat for dinner. The man can't be far away. We'll use Laird Malcomb's dogs, and we'll have him tonight, but until we do, promise you'll stay here."

Amber had barely nodded yes when everyone rushed out of the room and she was alone.

How long would it take to catch the man so that Tomas would come back here to this room where she would be waiting?

Ceithir Deug (14)

Tomas was exhausted. It was still dark, but morning wasn't far away. He took the spiral stone stairs two at a time, thinking that perhaps he could get a little bit of sleep before he had to wake up and be on duty supervising the guards down at the docks inside the underground palace.

One of the guards on the floor of the castle where his bedroom was nodded at him in passing, and Tomas nodded back. Was that an amused smile on the man's face? What was that about?

Finally at the door to his room, he pushed it open, dropping his kilt to the floor as he did...

And there was Amber in his bed.

He sighed.

Careful not to rock the bed and wake her up, he crawled in beside her, dreading what it would be like if she woke up and pulled away from him. He didn't care, of course. He had a girlfriend. But it would be, you know, awkward if Amber were to wake up with a horrified face at seeing him in the bed with her and pull away. That was all.

Except she did wake up. And she didn't pull away.

She reached over and pulled his arm around her, pulling him close behind her like a cloak of safety against the evil cruel world.

And it was just reflex that made him hold her close. A protective reflex. Because she was probably afraid, being here all alone in this strange room not knowing what was happening with... her friends.

They cuddled, and a peace came over him such as he hadn't known in seven years. Not only peace. Something else was lurking under the surface of it. Something he tamped down so that it wouldn't catch flame. He was with Sulis. Amber was just a friend who needed his protection, and he was only doing what any friend would do.

But her voice was throaty and sexy with sleep when she spoke.

"Did you get him?"

He sighed, which pressed him closer to her. She caressed his arm in response, and it felt good. His mouth went to kiss the back of her head, but he stopped it in time. Just an old habit, you know, from when they used to be together.

He cleared his throat

"No. And we searched the whole town. The dogs only just caught Lachlan's scent an hour ago. They followed him all the way out to Port Patrick. We had to turn back or else their barking would've woken everyone there. The good news is it looks like he's taking ship and going somewhere else. Good riddance."

She squeezed his arm and shook it a little in victory.

"That is good news."

He nodded his head, and because her head was so close in front of his on the pillow, it was as if he were nuzzling her, but he hadn't meant to.

"Yeah, so you don't have to be afraid."

She drew his arm more tightly around her.

"I'm not afraid, not now that you're here."

His heart swelled when she said that. Just because, you know, it was good to feel he had helped her.

It was quiet for so long that he thought she'd gone back to sleep. Fat chance of him getting to sleep with his front pressed against her back like this. It didn't mean anything except that he was a healthy male and she was an attractive...

Never mind. He was with Sulis. He couldn't be thinking that way.

As gently as he could, he put some of the covers between their middles. He didn't want to wake Amber. But then after a while, she spoke again, so softly he could have pretended he was asleep and didn't hear.

"Tomas?"

But what was the fun in that?

"Yeah?"

"What happened on your eighteenth birthday? Why did you leave me? I worried about you, and I've missed you something awful. Tell me you had a good reason."

Her words hurt. He had tried to put out of his mind how he must've hurt her.

"I was trying to protect you, Amber. I was sworn to secrecy about all this, the time travel stuff. I guess it's kind of pointless to be silent on it now. But the answer to your question is a long story."

"I'm not going anywhere."

Good, because I like having you here.

Keep talking though, or you'll lose control of yourself, Tomas.

His hand started combing through her long dark hair while he thought on how to introduce his dad's story about Sean MacGregor. It didn't seem anything but friendly, though, so he let it keep smoothing through her silky tresses.

"You know how authentic everyone always says my dad is, his Gaelic accent and his skill at sword-fighting and even the expressions on his face?"

"Yeah. Yeah, it's like he's from…" She raised up and turned her head to look him in the eye, and she had a 'Eureka!' look on her face. "Oh my… He is from back in the past, isn't he."

He gathered her close again so that she would lie down. Looking into her eyes felt just as wrong as kissing her would have felt. No, that wasn't quite true. Looking into her eyes made him want to kiss her, and he mustn't do that. He was with Sulis.

"Yep. My dad was born in the 1520s on the MacGregor lands in Glen Strae, Scotland, near Kilchurn Castle... It's so strange. The MacGregor name doesn't even exist yet in this time we're in now, you know."

"It doesn't?"

"No. The name comes from Viking Lord Donnchadh Beag's son Griogair, and he's just a boy right now."

"That is weird. No wonder Seumas looks at Tavish and you so oddly sometimes."

"Well, Seumas knows everything."

Her muscles flexed.

"He does? Who else knows, Eileen?"

"No one else."

She relaxed again.

"Anyway, so your dad is from the 1500s in the Highlands. And he's a time traveler. So why did that make you leave me without saying a word, and without your parents telling me anything? I looked up to your parents, you know. I thought they were my friends. Losing them hurt almost as much as losing you."

He stroked her hair some more, but this time tenderly, trying to soothe her.

"They still are your friends, Amber. In their own way, they were protecting all of us by keeping this time travel stuff from us until we were old enough to see the sense in keeping it a secret, but I do think they should have told us about the curse earlier."

"What curse?"

"Well, Dad wasn't a time traveler by choice. Neither is Tavish."

"Sort of like I didn't travel here by choice."

"You didn't?"

"No. No, I was... wandering around in the underground castle that same night after you stopped Lachlan from running me off the cliff, and suddenly I just got dizzy. I didn't know what was happening to me, Tomas."

He squeezed her tight, remembering with shame how impatient he'd been with her when he found her in this time in her modern clothes.

"I'm so sorry for how I acted when you got here to this time."

"You're forgiven."

He relaxed his hold on her until they were just cuddling again.

"Anyway, Dad — and now Tavish has taken his place — they are servants of the druid family whose ancestor enslaved one of our ancestors, a certain Sean MacGregor, who was stupid enough to have insurmountable gambling debts." He told her the whole story.

She pounded the bed with her fist.

"What an idiot."

Tomas laughed in spite of himself. She had always said exactly what was on her mind. It was one of the things he... one of the reasons she was his friend.

"Yeah, he was an idiot. Sean chose

enslavement voluntarily, and for that reason we've been told there is very little chance of our family ever escaping the curse that druid put on us through Sean."

He stopped there and was quiet for a while, letting that sink in. That was the part that he and his brothers and his nephews had argued the hardest against when their parents had told them the story. 'Can't we just break this curse?' they had insisted when told their girlfriends might have children who would be enslaved, if they married them. 'There has to be a way.'

Amber didn't argue, though.

"I see," was all she said. It made him feel like a child, compared to her. Had she always been more mature than him?

Probably.

He resumed combing her long dark hair with his fingers.

"That was what my parents told us on our eighteenth birthday, me and Tavish. That, and the fact that with two others among the faire people, Dad was sent to our time by the druids he serves in order to make the faire authentic and a crowd pleaser and a moneymaker for the druids—"

She sat up and looked down at him.

"Wait, so your parents don't get to keep any of the money the faire makes? It all goes to the druids? Why don't they just quit? And why would you want to be a part of that, running the business end of it for the benefit of a bunch of druids? That's stupid, Tomas!"

He sat up in bed as well and took her hand, wiggling it to negate what she was thinking.

"No, it isn't like that anymore. I would never want to be a part of it if it were. No, now, our clan does get to keep most of the money. Dad and Mom and Peadar and Vange, they bargained with the druids. They think they got a good deal, but the curse is still intact, so not really. Every fourth-born son in our line still has to serve the druids if he lives to be twenty-five years old. In our immediate family, that's Tavish. He's the younger of us two. I came out first."

She laughed a little at that.

"I know. Do you realize how often you used to say that? Every time you wanted to win an argument with him, you'd bring that up, 'I came out first.'"

Her laughter did awkward things to the front of him. He turned around and pulled her close to his own back. She fit there like a glove. She always had. And the connection he felt with her now was just as strong as it had ever been.

He felt a pang of guilt. What about Sulis?

What about her.

She's pushy and arrogant and loud and obnoxious.

Has no manners whatsoever.

Worse, she belittles all the women and manipulates all the men. It's a wonder none of the women have punched her, she's so awful. Why on God's green earth am I with that... Just what is she, anyway? And what am I doing here playing Captain of the Guard when all I've ever wanted to do is help run the Renaissance Fairee that Mom & Dad built up to such a wonderful event and such a financial success?

Memories of Amber trying to tell him Sulis was a druid who had charmed him with magic came to him. He pondered them in the back of his mind while he enjoyed being here with Amber in the moment.

But he also decisively resolved some things.

When Sulis came back, he would break up with her. And he would leave this ruse of a life she had stuck him in and return to his own time and his real life. And once he was free of Sulis, he would ask Amber to join him.

But for now, we would enjoy this moment.

"Yeah, well... So anyway, that was why Tavish and I left you and Kelsey. We didn't want you to have to see your children enslaved to the druids."

She took a deep breath and let it out slowly.

"But in the modern world, there are ways to avoid having more than three kids."

"Vange tried that, but even in the modern world there are druids, and they have life magic, Amber. Vange was only going to have three kids, and look. She had two sets of twin boys."

"I'd like to see druidic magic work on someone who's had a hysterectomy. That would foil them for sure. But even if we did have a fourth son, this time travel thing's kind of fun."

He chuckled.

"Yeah, it kind of is, but now that I see it with clarity, being here in the past feels like playing at life rather than living life, even though I know for the people here, this is real life."

She smirked mockingly at him in a playful way.

"Wow, that was deep."

He raised his hands up like claws and put a crazed look in his eyes.

"Yeah? I'll show you deep. My fingers are going to go so deep into your sides that your laugh will wake up all the guards in the whole hallway."

She lay back and raised her knees up in front of her and lowered her hands to her sides in order to prevent him from tickling her, but he was familiar with these defenses. Every time she moved, he moved the opposite way and went in for the tickle.

Her giggles melted him though, and he stopped abruptly, sitting up above her and looking down at her long chocolate brown hair splayed on the pillow and her cheeks rosy with exertion and her soft brown eyes dancing with laughter.

"Amber, I was a fool to ever leave you."

With that, she stilled, and the look in her eyes turned from playfulness to an adoration so deep, it made him yearn to live up to it.

Còig Deug (15)

Tomas was snoring when Amber woke up.

She used the chamber pot, washed her face and hands, and went out in the hall and waved to the first guard she saw.

"Tomas was oot late last night with the dogs, hunting Lachlan the Dark. I ken he's supposed tae hae duty now, but can ye let him sleep? He truly does need the rest."

The guard must have been a dullard, because he just kind of stood there gaping at her, not answering.

She would just have to assume he'd pass on her message. She needed to get out of this castle and talk to Kelsey. It was late enough in the morning that she knew her friend would already be at the weaver shop.

Amber passed through the great hall on her way out in the hopes that someone would feed her. Sure enough, a serving woman handed her a plate of eggs and ham and beans, which she ate up quickly, she was so hungry from staying up late and sleeping in.

All the way to the weaver shop, she rehearsed what she was going to say to Kelsey. It was hard, because she had felt so close to Tomas last night. It had been as if they never parted and were still together.

But they weren't together. He was still with Sulis.

Kelsey took one look at Amber's face as she entered the weaver shop and handed her work to Sasha, who set it down next to her own and gave Amber a sympathetic look.

Kelsey walked over and gave Amber a hug, then turned to Eileen and Sasha.

"Amber and I have an errand to run."

The pretty blonde weaver looked from Amber to Kelsey and back again with a smirk on her face and opened her mouth to say something.

But before she could, Deirdre came running over to Amber and stopped with her hands on her hips.

"I want tae go with ye. Ye are na gaun'ae run errands. Ye are just gaun'ae go walking aroond and talking, aren't ye. Probably even buy one o Maureen's sticky buns and eat it all by yerself. I want tae go."

Amber was feeling guilty for not wanting to take the little girl. She was so darn cute, and she had helped Amber find the tinker's booth...

But the girl's mother put an end to her demands.

"Deirdre Anne, ye go right back tae yer washing and close yer mouth this instant. Ye dinna speak tae grown ones that way." Eileen turned to Kelsey. "I am sae sorry. I dinna ken what got intae her. Go on with ye." She made shooing gestures with her hands as she sat back down at her spinning wheel.

To Amber's amazement, Deirdre went and did exactly what she was told without any complaints. Her brothers were helping her, and their little baby sister sat watching with her thumb in her mouth.

As Kelsey walked Amber toward the door, she made a face that said, 'Yikes. I'm glad we're getting out of here for a little while, aren't you?'

Amber nodded, and together they waved goodbye to the others.

Instead of walking around town as Deirdre assumed they would, Amber walked Kelsey straight past the castle and out toward the cliffs, where the noisy ocean would prevent their voices from carrying to anyone.

And then she looked Kelsey in the eye and bared her soul, as tears came and showed just how upset she was.

"Yesterday Eileen told me about a local enchantress named Elsbeth, and I went to see her. That's what I was doing out in the woods when Lachlan found me and Tomas found Lachlan. Kelsey, Elsbeth says the only thing that can break the curse of false love is true love. Last night after Tomas came back to his room, I thought we had true love. But when I woke up this morning, I realized he's still with Sulis. Nothing has changed. Soon as she comes back, he'll be that zombie again. I can't take it."

Kelsey caught her up in a hug.

"Whoa, whoa, whoa. What happened?"

Amber brushed her tears away with one of her huge voluminous linen sleeves.

"Nothing and everything. We spent most of this morning spooning."

Kelsey tried to hide a gasp.

"Did you..."

Amber shook her head violently no while she fought the choking sobs that wanted to prevent her from talking.

"We just cuddled and talked and got caught up, Kelsey. And it was like we'd never been apart. And that's even worse than if... I feel so close to him, but he's still with Sulis. Nothing happened at all — and everything happened. I mean I'm feeling so close to him, but I shouldn't be. I almost wish I had never come here to Scotland. Having him so close to me again just brings home how much it hurts that he doesn't want to be with me, not in the way I want. I'm trying, Kelsey. I really am trying to save him from that B witch. But if he doesn't come around soon, I'm going to ask Tavish to take me back to the modern world so I can move on without Tomas. It kills me to do it, but I won't have my heartstrings pulled by someone who isn't sure how to feel."

She dissolved into sobs then, grateful that her friend was there.

Kelsey gently patted her back.

"He'll come around soon. I know he will. He loves you, even if he doesn't know it right now. Don't give up yet. Stay just a little bit longer, because I think all he needs is just a little more time. We can't let that B witch win without a fight. Remind him that he loves you. Give him a fighting chance to choose you."

Amber wanted to believe Kelsey, wanted to with every fiber of her being. Her heart begged her to believe. It was everything she had ever hoped for. But her head kept telling her to guard her heart and withdraw before her heart broke beyond repair.

The two of them walked slowly back toward the weaver shop. All that awaited them there was boring work. Or so she thought. Right up until she found Tomas standing outside the weaver shop holding the bridal of a horse and grinning at her in invitation to go for a ride with him.

Filled with elation, she ran to him without even looking back at Kelsey, whom she vaguely heard laughing behind her.

Amber had ridden horseback with Tomas many times, and before she knew it, she was on the horse behind him and they were galloping away from the town with her laughing with delight.

Once more, she had her arms around him and her head pressed against his back, soaking in the closeness of him — albeit through far more clothing than there had been between them last night.

This was what life was meant to be like! Galloping through the Highlands — green grass, gray rocky hills, soaring cloudy skies — while holding on tight to the man she loved. It was so wonderful, she didn't even dare ask him where they were going.

This probably wasn't a date. He probably had someplace he needed to take her for her safety. And she was glad he was concerned. That was a good sign, right? It meant he cared. He had even admitted that. She sure as heck didn't want to ask and find out for sure this wasn't a date. Sometimes, silence really was golden.

Live in the moment. Wasn't that what they always said?

It would be difficult to talk on a galloping horse anyway. Best to just enjoy the feeling of closeness, the thudding of their bodies together as the horse bounced off the rocks and dirt and rocks again. To count the trees in the forest they rode through, or the different kinds of bird chirps that could be heard amongst the branches.

But mostly just to feel him against her and be happy.

They rode close together like this for half an hour or so.

But all things must pass, and she felt the pang

of sadness when he slowed down.

Their halt wasn't all bad, though. He had stopped the horse at the top of a long gradual hill that sloped down to the ocean. It was sandy down there. He climbed down, tied the horse to a tree, and then handed her down.

"We'll leave him here where he can graze."

Tomas was still holding her hand, and it felt so right — but a beach awaited them. With one accord, they ran down to the sea. The weather here in Scotland was much too cold for swimming, but this was nice. Far away from everyone else, with only the waves and the wind looking on or listening.

Their eyes met, and they smiled together as they shared a sense of wonder at their surroundings.

But a dark question took hold of her, and she searched his face for the answer, a bit worried about what she would find.

"Have you been here before?"

But his eyes reassured her.

"Yeah, but only with fellow guards. This isn't the type of place she likes, but I know you like the beach. And Amber, I broke up with Sulis this morning."

"Say that again?" She knocked imaginary sand out of her ear. "I think I'm hearing things."

He laughed.

"I broke up with Sulis this morning."

"Really?"

"Really."

"How did she take it? Was anyone else

around? Does everyone know?"

He laughed again and smiled his handsome smile at her.

"Oh, yeah. Everyone knows. They all know I'm out with you now, too."

She smiled at him in genuine enjoyment then.

She was on a date with Tomas. He was making an effort to spend time with her outside the fortress where he had the excuse of keeping her safe. Hope swelled in her heart. And she almost grabbed him and kissed him until the sun was setting and it was too cold to stay outdoors.

But she would still wait for him to make the first move. He would want to. That was the sort of man he was: a manly one. She wouldn't have him any other way.

He took her hand in his and led her along the line where the sand met the cliff.

"See that little cranny in the rocks that looks like a clown?"

She tried her best to enjoy taking this slow and have a good time and appreciate the small things. She really did.

"It does!"

They walked along the cliff line some more, commenting on this little nook and that little cranny, this flower or that fern. And still all she could think about was grabbing him and sticking her tongue in his mouth, dueling tongues with him, then going home and telling her parents they were back together.

It was a sunny day, and they pointed out where they could see buildings sticking up on the shoreline of distant Ireland across the sea. And she imagined what it would be like to move to Australia with him and help run the faire. So exciting! The life she had always wanted but never dared to dream about...

They picked up seashells.

Combed designs in the sand with sticks for the waves to wash away.

Watched sand crabs burrow.

Built a sandcastle.

And midway through their date, she was able to stop dreaming of their future and just live in the moment. She had a wonderful time. All the while they also played a game of tag, where one would run and the other would chase. It was how they were accustomed to being together, having last dated when they were teens.

A few hours later when they had completed their circle around their private oasis, Tomas hugged her close with the sea breeze whistling through their hair and the seagulls calling out as they soared in circles through the air overhead and Ireland gradually disappearing into the mist across the sea.

And then his lips were on hers.

It was a spontaneous kiss, born out of delight at the scenery and how fun it was to be exploring this together, playing together.

Wanting more, Amber grabbed ahold of him with a reckless abandon born from wanting him so much this past week and not being able to act on it. She poured her heart into kissing him back, opening her mouth to deepen the kiss and holding him close to show him just how much she'd missed him, just how much she loved him.

But he didn't respond in kind.

No, his arms dropped to his sides and the look on his face was...

Well, it was a look of bafflement, really.

Amber's blood boiled.

The stupid spell was still getting in the way!

She kicked sand onto Tomas's legs to try and snap him out of his stupor.

"Tell me right now, do you want to be with me, or Sulis?"

He didn't even answer her, just stood there with his forehead wrinkled, not saying anything.

That was it. She was so pissed off, she was back up the hill in no time and on top of the horse and galloping away without him.

Sia Deug (16)

Well, this was awkward. She was riding up to the stable on the horse before she remembered that guard she'd told that Tomas needed his sleep. And this was the smallest of small towns she had ever been to. Everyone and their mother likely knew now that she had slept in Tomas's room with him — before he broke up with Sulis.

So now on top of everything else, her face was beet red when she approached the stable hand, an older man who vaguely resembled her uncle. Great.

Quick as she could, she dismounted and handed the man the reins, then turned to leave.

But of course she didn't get away that easily.

"Hey now, lass. This is the horse Tomas took oot. Where is he?"

~*~

Tomas was both relieved and embarrassed when one of his guards showed up on the trail back to Laird Malcomb's castle from Maidenhead Bay — leading an extra horse. Mostly, he was glad to get back in the saddle after walking for an hour. No, mostly he was angry at Amber for leaving him in that embarrassing situation.

Maybe he was a little angry at himself. One moment he'd been kissing Amber — and loving it. The next moment, he'd been standing there like a simpleton, unable to decide what to do or say, just simply stupefied.

What the blazes had come over him? Why had he let himself hurt yet again the woman who had left her whole life behind to fly to him?

As the horses' hooves clopped over the mossy roots of the forest, this question kept running through his mind. He found that he suspected Sulis had something to do with it — but he couldn't say why. It was just there, the thought that she would do something if she found out he was kissing Amber. He certainly didn't have any love in his heart for Sulis.

Quite the opposite, really.

He had ridden up to the stable and dismounted and was handing the stable hand his reins when the older man spoke to him.

"The lass what stole yer horse is being held in yer chamber."

Hearing this, Tomas's body went rigid, ready to run to her and fight for her freedom. And then terrible visions came to his mind.

"They didna hurt her, did they?"

To Tomas's relief, the stable hand shook his head no, although he did have a teasing look in his eyes, as if he were bursting to ask Tomas how Amber had gotten his horse from him. Thankfully, the man had more sense than to ask.

"They await yer orders."

Tomas breathed a sigh of relief. He had to try and remember how brutal this place could be. He didn't like it at all. He should have gone after Amber and not let her return here alone. What was wrong with him?

"I thank ye."

The gray stone hallways and stairways of the castle whizzed by along with several people he merely nodded at on his quest to get to Amber before they did hurt her. What was the punishment for horse thievery in these times? He ran harder. It might be death.

Heaving for breath, he pushed into his chamber, ready to throw out anyone who had lifted a finger against her.

But he found Amber sitting in the one chair in the room, laughing and talking with the two guards who stood on either side of the door.

"Och, I dae wish ye could hae seen him. Head tae toe in mud he was, and chasing the rest o us aboot like a moor monster! Och, there ye are, Tomas. Ye got here faster than I thought ye would. I was just telling these guards about the fun times we used tae hae together in oor village."

At first, the guards smiled at him in appreciation of her story, but then they seemed to remember themselves, and they stood up to attention, looking like they were afraid of reprimand.

Why were they afraid of him?

Doing his best to put them at ease, Tomas smiled back and rolled his eyes to show them that yes, Amber's tale was true, and he didn't like to think about it.

"Ye are dismissed. Leave us."

At this, the guards definitely smirked at him as if to say they knew exactly why he wanted to be alone with this pretty lass.

He put the air of command on his face and raised his chin at them.

They got the message and beat it out of there quickly, closing the door behind them.

Tomas turned to Amber.

"I can't believe you left me there to walk home."

Amber shrugged, not looking at all sheepish. No, she looked more like the wolf. She even gave him a few notes of sharp derisive laughter. She got up while she spoke, and paced the room, alternately making wild gestures and giving him heated stares.

"Are you kidding? You deserved it. You kissed me, Tomas. All I did was respond to you — and then you looked at me like I was nuts. That's no way to treat a stranger, let alone an old friend who cares about you, unlike... the people you choose to spend your time with. I really don't get it, Tomas. You're so hot and cold. I want to believe you care about me, and sometimes I do believe it. And then you go and do something like pull away when I'm kissing you. Your embarrassment at having to be picked up by the guards is nothing compared to how that felt for me."

Her ferocity amazed and attracted him like nothing else ever had, and her determination to get what she wanted, because that was him. A warm spot heated up in his heart at that thought.

But she was trying to push past him and get to the door.

"I can't stand to be here in this room with you one more second, Tomas. You need to make up your mind who you're going to be with and quit playing with me like I'm some toy you keep to the side until your woman comes back to you."

What?

He put his arms around her.

"Amber, I already told you. I broke up with Sulis. She is out of my life once and for all. Don't go."

She squeezed him tight then.

"Oh Tomas, really?"

He deepened their embrace.

"Really."

And then he gave her the loving kiss he should've returned earlier.

~*~

Amber awoke with a start. What the heck was

she doing here? This room still smelled like Sulis. Sure, he had broken up with her, but he hadn't said that she and he were together. He had simply kissed her and expected her to stay with him, with no assurance it meant anything beyond warming his bed for the night. There wasn't even the excuse that she was here for her safety, now that Lachlan had sailed away.

How could she have been so stupid?

Glancing over to make sure he was deep asleep — which he was — she pulled herself together and hightailed it to Eileen's house, not looking at any of the guards or the few townsfolk who were out and about at the crack of dawn. She didn't want to see the pity on their faces. Pity for the woman who was the plaything and not the wife or even the girlfriend.

She would wake Kelsey up and make her go get Tavish so he could take her back to her own time. If Tomas really did want to be with her, then he would come back to her. And right now, all she could think was fat chance of that happening.

He had admitted that life here in the past seemed like playing pretend. Well, she wasn't going to pretend with him. She was either his partner in real life, or just a memory. And he had better come back soon and say so. Seven years was all the time she had to waste, and that time had already been wasted.

Not about to knock and wake everyone up, she opened Eileen's door as quietly as she could — and saw that the place had been ransacked, torn to bits. Heart thudding in her chest with worry, she searched all the rooms, but not a soul was to be found, dead or alive. She needed to go tell the guards! But a hand came from behind her to cover her mouth, and a sudden spell washed over her, knocking Amber out cold.

Seachd Deug

Amber was dreaming. Kelsey's face kept appearing in the shadows of the woods. Her friend was talking, but no sound came out. Amber cupped her hand around her ear and shook her head, trying to tell Kelsey she couldn't hear her. But her friend just kept talking. She had an urgent look on her face, as if what she was saying was critically important. Amber strained to hear, but she couldn't.

Gradually, the dream faded away until Amber was aware of a cold hard stone surface pressing up against her back and head. Her arms were stretched back around the slender cold stone and tightly secured at her wrists. She could move them up and down a little, and when she did, she felt the leather cord that tied them together scraping against the stone she leaned against.

Admitting she was awake meant she could listen to the voices a few dozen feet away in front of her. At first, she just heard a man's voice asking questions, in modern-day English. But then a woman started answering, and she had a Southern accent. Sulis.

"I'm truly glad you want to help me with the ritual, but remember, it is far more important for you to keep an eye out in case someone comes."

"What should I do if someone does happen along?"

"Don't you say a thing. Just kill them before they know what hit them."

"Yes, Mistress."

Amber gasped and cautiously cracked her eyes open the tiniest bit.

She was in a church graveyard, tied to a gravestone. It was early evening, just about dark but not too cold yet. She saw a little church, a bunch of gravestones, and a forest all around them with trees so thick she felt walled-in. Owls hooted in the trees, lending that spooky atmosphere she had felt near Elsbeth's without the good enchantress nearby to allay her fears.

Spread all over her clothes were flowers, and at her feet, brambles were heaped up. Something prickly rested on top of her head. She tried to shake it off, but it was snug.

And not thirty feet away, Sulis and Lachlan tended a big fire in their white robes.

Amber wanted to scream and have someone

come help her, but the druids were the only two people near enough to hear her. And she sure enough didn't want their attention. Instead, she kept working the leather cord up and down on the other side of the gravestone.

Lachlan sounded whiney as he went on.

"You know I would do anything for you, Sulis, unlike some people."

Sulis stopped tending the fire and turned her deceptively pretty face to the other druid. She took his hand in hers and softened her tone when she next spoke.

"Oh sugar, you know I was just dating Tomas in order to put him under the spell."

She tooted a derisive laugh.

"It was so cute of him to break up with me, like that would make any difference. He'll still be a wonderful slave once the ritual is complete and the spell takes hold completely. I have him set up as Captain of the guard, you know. I'll be able to loot all the relics in this time, before that busybody Kelsey and her modern-day client can ever get ahold of them."

The big sleeve of Sulis's white linen robe billowed as she gestured over toward Amber.

"Only recently did I realize someone was preventing all that."

Lachlan laughed that evil laugh he had. It gave Amber the shivers before he even spoke.

"Glad I was able to help in capturing that someone for you."

Sulis raised her chin and stuck a pose.

"I really don't get what he sees in her. I'm

much prettier."

Apparently emboldened by her obvious fish for compliments, Lachlan dropped his voice lower to something that was supposed to sound sexy, but it just made Amber roll her eyes.

"Of course you are. You are perfection."

Sulis laughed at that in her sickeningly sweet false modest way that made Amber throw up a little in her mouth. And then the two of them kissed.

Amber scraped the cord against the back of the headstone as hard as she could.

But Sulis made quick work of kissing Lachlan back into submission mode.

"All right, let's get on with the ritual. Once this is done, nothing will stand in the way of Tomas's complete obedience to me. Hand me that rag to catch the blood, will you?"

Blood?

At that, Amber's eyes popped open wide.

Sulis was coming toward her with evil in her eyes, holding a dagger.

Wait... was that...? It was!

Sulis was brandishing the very same dagger that had been tucked in Tavish's belt after he had left with a different dagger that day in modern times in the underground palace. How had Sulis gotten the dagger?

Oh.

Kelsey had mentioned something about giving it to... The druids.

Amber started trembling.

Because behind Sulis, Tomas was rushing out

of a hiding place to stop the druidess. He was close enough that he was going to catch her. He was also close enough that he had heard everything — and seen Sulis and Lachlan kissing.

Tomas's arms came out. Two more seconds and he would grab hold of Sulis's waist and tackle her.

But Lachlan was running toward Tomas, and he tackled Tomas before Tomas reached Sulis.

Ochd Deug (18)

Amber feared for Tomas's life as he wrestled with Lachlan on the graveyard grass. Because the druids didn't fight fair. Someone had used magic to knock Amber out at Eileen's house, and it must've been Lachlan, kidnapping her for his slave-mistress.

But Amber had to tear her eyes away from Tomas and Lachlan's fight.

Because Sulis was still running toward her with that nasty dagger sticking out in front of her. The druidess's white robes billowed out behind her like flags waving in the wind, and there was a crown of leaves and brambles and flowers on her head. Her hair was down, wild and frizzy. She held the dagger in her right hand and a rag to collect Amber's blood in her left.

Amber furiously dragged the leather cord up against the back of the gravestone as hard as she could — and it snapped. Just in time, too. Sulis was lunging at her with the dagger. Purely by instinct, Amber brought her arms forward just in time to tear the dagger out of the witch's hands. The impact threw Sulis off balance, and she went tumbling through the grass and fall leaves.

But Amber's attention was riveted on the dagger.

For as soon as she touched it, the dagger began speaking in her mind.

"Wull met, sweet lass. I am Galdus, king o auld, now residing inside this dagger. Sae long as ye possess me, ye will hae my undying loyalty. I am sae glad ye rescued me from that evil druidess. I dinna want tae serve the likes o her. Howsoever, I will gladly serve ye. And tae that end, I dae tell ye now: in but a moment she will get up and come throttle ye with her hands — unless ye stab her in the heart with me. Dae it! Dae it now!"

Glancing over at Sulis, Amber saw the truth in what the dagger had told her. The druidess was getting up. She seemed none the worse for her fall, and she had threatened to drain Amber's blood in order to safeguard her false-love spell on Tomas.

Galdus spoke up again.

"'Tis tae late tae go after her. Lie here in wait with me prepared, and as soon as ye see the whites o her eyes, raise me up and she will land right on me and impale herself. Ye dinna hae tae fash about having her blood on yer hands, for twill be her own intent that does her in. Aye, 'tis a good way tae go aboot it. Good on ye for waiting till the evil lass came toward ye. Bide a bit. Bide a bit. She's a coming. Now!"

Amber raised Galdus up just as Sulis dove on her. The weight of the woman pushed the dagger down toward the ground, and Amber's arm was against the grass when she felt the dagger go in. And then the weight was gone.

Amber opened her eyes to find that Sulis had dissolved into a pile of ashes: white robe, garland of flowers, and all. Relief washed over Amber, allowing all of her limbs to relax and her heart to calm. A deep breath filled her lungs.

But her relief was short-lived.

Looking for Tomas, she saw that Lachlan had indeed knocked her love out with one of his evil spells. And the druid was holding up another dagger over Tomas's heart, chanting an evil incantation.

Galdus didn't waste any time.

"Get up, lass! Get up and go stab me intae his back from behind. He is na worth the wee bit o fashing I sense in ye at the thought o backstabbing anyone. He is na deserving o yer fashing, lass. Just dae it. Dae it now!"

Amber wasn't a fighter by any stretch of the imagination. Oh sure, she dished out snark whenever she could find a receptacle for it. But those were words. The thought of a physical fight? Yeah, that usually had her crawling away to hide like the coward she knew she was.

But that was Tomas over there in peril.

Adrenaline pumped through her veins, giving her just the burst of energy she needed to jump up, run over, and stab the white-robed druid in the back before he plunged his dagger into Tomas's heart.

As soon as Amber stabbed Lachlan, he too dissolved into a pile of ashes: white robes, garland of brambles, and all. Only this time it happened right before Amber's eyes. It wasn't a gradual thing. No. One second she was plunging Galdus into a man's back, and the next second the man's ashes were falling to the ground in a heap.

Amber didn't care about that.

Eyes blurry with sudden tears and throat choked up with sobbing, she cast Galdus aside and threw herself to the ground next to Tomas, despairing that he would never wake up from Lachlan's evil spell, now that the druid was gone.

In the firelight, Amber saw Tomas lying stock still on his back in his billowy sleeved linen shirt and his scratchy wool kilt on top of the green, green grass with his gorgeous face upward toward the gray Scottish sky. He looked so peaceful lying there among the gravestones — too peaceful.

Amber leaned over her love's face, trying to feel any breath coming out of him.

She felt none.

Grabbing him by the shoulders, she shook

him.

When that produced nothing, she dropped down and hugged him to her.

"Tomas? Tomas, wake up. The evil B witch is gone, and so is her minion. I'm here free and whole, and I love you, Tomas. I love you with all my heart. I always have."

He didn't stir.

She felt no heartbeat in his chest.

She waited there holding her breath, with her tears falling on his face.

Nothing happened.

Amber couldn't blame the next impulse on Galdus, for she had cast him aside, and now that she wasn't touching the dagger, her mind was free of its urgings.

Tenderly, lovingly, she kissed those lips that were cold with the promise of death, pouring into the kiss all the love she had.

~*~

Certain she was delusional, Amber felt Tomas respond to her kiss. Her desperate imagination had him holding her tight with his arms and turning his head so that their mouths locked together and dueling her tongue with his. She didn't care if it was just her imagination. She was going to enjoy this last moment of warmth and joy and pleasure with the man she loved.

So she did. She held him close and soaked in the nearness of him one last time.

And then she knew she needed to let go of this dream and embrace reality. It wasn't healthy for her to stay in this fantasy for too long. With despair in her heart, she withdrew from Tomas.

But the fantasy clung.

She heard his voice, soft and caring and loving — the way she had been longing to hear it for seven years.

"Can't you bear to look at me? I guess I can't blame you after my idiocy with Sulis. But I want you to know that I love you, Amber. I've always loved you. Please tell me you came to rescue me because you love me too. Tell me we're going to spend the rest of our lives together. I'm so sorry I was deluded by Sulis. I was there the whole time inside my head, and once you showed up, I wanted to break free. But I couldn't fight my way out of it. You did that for me, Amber. You broke through the prison I was in, deep inside my own mind. I loved you even before, but the love I have for you now knows no bounds. I should have known it would be you who would save me from that prison. Will you ever forgive me? I know it must have hurt, you seeing me with her. I wouldn't blame you if you didn't forgive me, but I'm begging. Please forgive me, Amber."

She must have been holding on to the fantasy in order for his voice to come to her so clearly and so realistically. But with a heavy sigh she opened her eyes.

And gasped.

He was right there, sitting on the grass. Her face must have shown her confusion and doubt.

Because he laughed.

"That is so not the look I expected to see on your face when I declared my undying love."

She felt herself laughing, but inside she was still not willing to believe this was real.

"Any moment, I'll wake up and this will have been the most wonderful dream ever — well, except for the part where we both almost got killed by crazed druids."

It was at that point she realized this was real, because his face turned to a look of anguish.

"Amber I'm so sorry — just so, so sorry about everything... Leaving you when I found out about the MacGregor curse, and letting Sulis take control of me, and being so rude to you when you got here to Laird Malcomb's castle, and—"

She grabbed him and shut him up with a kiss. She made it the best one she had ever given him. They made out for all they were worth.

~*~

When Amber woke up on a bed of grass in Tomas's arms, he kissed her tenderly and then smiled in reluctance and gestured at the sun coming up over the church.

"We should be getting back."

She scrunched up her nose at him.

"Yeah, we probably should."

"Are you ready?"

"I guess so."

He got up and pulled her up, then brushed the grass off her long skirts and turned around so she could brush the grass off his kilt.

"We'll have plenty more opportunities to do this."

"You had better stick to that promise," she said in a teasing way, because experience with men told her they didn't like being scolded by their women.

But he gave her a sincere look.

"I will."

He threw his arm around her and started to walk her away from the almost-gruesome scene.

But on impulse, she went and snatched up the bag of Sulis and Lachlan's things — and found a rag inside to grab up Galdus with, then threw him in the bag as well.

Tomas reached to take the bag from her, but she smiled her best 'I can manage' smile, so he threw his arm over her shoulders and started them down the road with the birds chirping to greet the new day.

Naoi Deug (19)

It took two hours to walk back to Laird Malcolm's castle. Amber was relieved to find that Tomas knew the way, so they had two hours in which to plan their future together. They would stay on at the dig with Tavish and Kelsey for a month so that Amber could get Kelsey on her feet with the cataloging and such, and then Amber and Tomas would be off to Australia to learn how to run the business side of the Renaissance Fairee. It was going to be an even better future than Amber had ever dreamed it could be.

When they got close to the castle along the cliff path from Port Patrick, they heard music playing and people talking and laughing. Amber looked over at Tomas with a question in her eyes. He looked back at her and shrugged.

To Amber's shock, the first person to greet them was Tomas and Tavish's mom, Emily. Wearing her Renaissance Fairee costume — which Amber now realized must have been made in 1540 — she ran out from the castle town to grab them both together in a big hug.

"I knew ye were all right. And afore ye ask, aye, everyone here is all right as wull. Kelsey and her friends had already left for the weaver shop afore Eileen's house was ransacked—"

But even though Amber had come to Scotland to meet up with the woman's son, she couldn't wrap her mind around seeing her old guild-mistress from the faire again after seven years of being shunned by her. She stood off, pleased that Tomas stood off with her.

"Emily? What are ye doing here?"

Emily smiled at her in a knowing way, looking at Tomas's arm around her waist with a motherly gleam in her eye. It was an accepting look. In fact it was a little teasing.

"Why, I'm here for the big occasion. Tavish and Kelsey decided tae join in on Seumas & Sasha and Albert & Eileen's double wedding and make it a triple. And 'tis na just me who's here. Look."

Amber looked over toward the music to see that tables had been set up outside between the castle and the cliff. A small outdoor chapel had also been set up nearby, and a monk was standing ready with a glass of wine in his hand, smiling and tapping his feet to the music.

Half of her and Tomas's gang of friends from the fair sat around a table together, joking and laughing: Tavish and Kelsey, of course, and also Tavish and Tomas's aunt and uncle Vange and Peadar with their sons, who were Tomas and Tavish's cousins: Mike, Gabe, Jeff, and John—the John who hadn't deserted his girlfriend like all the others had, but who had broken up with Jaelle six months ago, back in their own time.

Emily caught Amber's eye and gave her and Tomas a mischievous grin. "Maybe the two of you would like to join in and get married too?"

That did it.

Amber was on the defensive again.

But she was guarding her heart.

Marrying Tomas was what she wanted more than anything in the world. Not daring to say anything and chase him away again, she just looked at him and tried her best to show in her eyes what she was feeling inside.

He raised his eyebrows at her.

"I'm game if ye are."

How dare he be teasing in a time like this? She went to pull away from him.

But he must have caught on to what she was thinking, and she melted into him when he took her in his arms and hugged her tight.

"I'm serious. Seven years was a long enough time tae wait tae be with ye. I want tae stop waiting. I want the rest o oor lives tae start now — and what better time tae get marrit then when

211

my whole family is already here?"

Wait, that wasn't fair. She playfully shoved him.

"Easy for ye tae say. Yer family is all here. But what aboot my family?"

He gave her a big smile and rocked back and forth with her in his arms, from foot to foot.

She sighed and relaxed into him. He knew her so well that he had seen right through her snark and realized she was saying yes.

Soft and rational though they were, his next words made her heart soar.

"We need tae make this legal, sae we'll dae it all again back at home where both o oor families can attend."

They stood there grinning at each other — him in a know-it-all way and her in a you-really-are-serious way — until she grabbed him and hugged him tight.

"I'm guessing I canna get oot o it that easily, eh?"

He held her close, getting several scandalized looks from the people passing by them on the path from Port Patrick.

In sotto voice, he said, "What's their problem?"

In kind, she said, "Ye know full wull the laws against public displays o affection. Tae them, we're criminals."

For some reason, this struck them as hilariously funny, and they broke out in laughter just as Tomas's dad, Dall, came over and put his arm around Emily.

Dall gathered the two of them into his hug as well, smiling with the same gleam in his eye as Emily had shown them. It said he had known all along they would get back together — and it welcomed Amber into their family. Amber's in-laws were going to be people she knew well. That should make everything a lot smoother.

Dall had caught most of what was going on with just a glance at Tomas's arm around Amber's waist, but he was at a loss as to what they were laughing about.

"What's sae funny?"

Emily winked at Amber.

"Tomas and Amber are gaun'ae make it a quadruple wedding."

Meanwhile, over at the tables, Tomas's family were calling his and Amber's names and making noises in a blatant attempt to get them to come join in on the revelry.

Dall smiled and gestured toward the party.

"Shall we?"

Amber beamed her biggest smile at him and grabbed Tomas's hand.

"Aye!"

They hadn't gone far when Kelsey ran out to join them, flapping her hands like the nervous wreck she obviously was, having known this was going to be her wedding day twelve hours longer than Amber had. She crashed into Amber and hugged her, then hugged Tomas too.

"Ye live! Thank all that's holy! What happened?"

Clutching the bag of druid stuff to her side,

Amber squinted at Kelsey as she dug through the bag with one hand, looking for Galdus.

"To make a long story short, Lachlan kidnapped me, Tomas followed him, and I turned Sulis and Lachlan into ash with this dagger —"

Kelsey gasped and lunged into Amber, closing the bag tight around her hand and stopping her search. When she spoke, it was to Dall and Emily as she grabbed Amber's hand and started dragging her toward the castle.

"We hae some aught urgent tae dae. Dinna begin the wedding withoot us."

Amber walked along quietly until they were out of earshot from everyone.

"What is it, Kelsey?"

"You can't keep that dagger. Someone else has an earlier claim to it, and I believe she'll know how to keep it safe — and secret."

At this, Amber felt rebellious. She hadn't given a thought to keeping the dagger until now, when someone was telling her she had to give it up. Suddenly, she wanted to insist on keeping it. It was special. It spoke in her mind!

Kelsey squeezed her hand and spoke softly.

"I know it's a special dagger, and you're probably getting really fond of it, but it's dangerous and distracting, and it will be much safer back here in the past, where no one knows where it is. There are those who will guess that you might have it and come after you. And if they find you with the dagger... Look, just trust me, okay? You're better off not keeping it." She took the bag off Amber's shoulder and put it on her own shoulder. "You can go back to the party. I'll be out in just a minute."

Amber was caught between the urge to be outraged that Kelsey had grabbed the bag off her shoulder and her common sense telling her that Kelsey was right and she should run far away from any druids wanting to come after her looking for the dagger.

"Uh, no. I'll stay with you, thank you very much."

As she followed Kelsey and the druid bag up the spiral stairs she had climbed with Tomas only a few days ago, Amber wondered who this person was that Kelsey was so sure would be careful to guard the secret of the dagger. Was it Laird Malcolm? He was a very responsible person of course, being the laird of a castle. Or maybe it would be the laird's wife. She wouldn't be nearly as busy as Laird Malcolm, not having to run a castle. What did the lady of a castle do, anyway? Amber had seen very little of Lady Malcolm.

She and Kelsey had finished climbing the stairs and were going down the stone hallway covered in tapestries toward the... nursery?

An older lady came out to greet them. Oh, maybe she was the one. Amber studied her.

The older lady smiled.

"Kelsey! Tae what dae I owe this pleasure on yer happiest o days?"

Kelsey smiled back.

"Hello, Isabel. This is my clanswoman Amber, who will also be getting marrit today. How about that? Might we borrow Deirdre? 'Tis the custom where we coome from tae hae a young lass carry flowers in the wedding ceremony, and she would be perfect."

Isabel turned around toward where Eileen's children were playing what looked like a game of King of the Hill.

"Deirdre! Come on ower, sweeting." She turned back to Kelsey and Amber. "What a lovely tradition. I would coome doon and watch, but these monkeys are much better off up here, and sae ye are as wull, ye ken?"

The children heard that and started making monkey noises and movements.

Kelsey laughed, and Amber joined in.

"Where on Earth did they ever see a monkey?"

Isabel looked at Amber as if she were daft.

"In the traveling menageries, o course. There hae been two coome round here since they were old enough tae remember — ah, perhaps yer clan lands are away from the sea, then, eh? I forget how much more o life we see here in a port town."

Soon, they had taken Deirdre back down the spiral staircase and through the bottom of the castle and out the door, where they had a brief time alone before they got to the wedding party.

Kelsey stopped and turned Deirdre round and fished Galdus out of the bag still inside the rag and covertly gave him to the little girl.

"Deirdre, Galdus is yers tae keep."

The excitement in the six-year-old's face was palpable, and Kelsey had to put her hand over Dierdre's mouth to keep her from screaming out in joy and excitement.

"He's yers tae keep, but ye must keep him in secret. Ye must na show him tae anybody, nor even let anybody see him. Ye ken?"

Deirdre nodded, and Kelsey helped her hide Galdus under her clothes before the three of them walked back to the wedding party tables and joined their friends.

But that little Deirdre was so clever. As soon as they sat down, she had something to say.

"How am I gaun'ae be a flower lass if I dinna hae any flowers tae bring?"

Kelsey gave Amber an amazed look and then turned to Sasha.

"Will ye help Deirdre pick some flowers tae carry during the wedding ceremony?"

Deirdre got up and ran over to Sasha, who held out her arms and then hugged the little girl, and the two of them ran off together where some flowers were growing near the cliffs.

The actual wedding ceremony was over in a whirl of activity before Amber could quite get a hold of what was going on, and when they were feasting afterwards, it was all fun and laughs because the pressure was off and they could just enjoy themselves and their friends' company.

Once all the food was eaten and quite a bit of wine had been drunk, and the men were relaxing with their pipes while the women turned toward each other and traded memories, Tomas squeezed Amber's arm as a sort of goodbye for a moment and got up and went over to Tavish's side of Kelsey.

Interesting. What was Tomas going to say to his brother?

To top it off, Tomas's face was all scrunched up with worry, and he didn't ask for his twin brother's attention, but rather just stood there quietly until Tavish noticed him and turned to him.

Tomas gestured, and with one accord, Tomas, Amber, Tavish, and Kelsey walked to the cliff, where the sound of the sea hitting the rocks would keep their voices from carrying back to the tables.

When Tomas finally spoke, a hush had come upon their group.

"Tavish, I've been under a terrible sense of envy for you ever since I found out about the curse and that you would be the one who got to time travel. I wanted to be the one. All I thought about was the fun of it and the adventure of it and what might be gained from it. I never once considered how awful it must be to have to answer to the druids as their slave. These past few months I've gotten a small taste of what you must be living with, and brother I've got to say I'm so, so sorry. You have it worse than I ever imagined or gave you credit for, and I'm here now to ask your forgiveness. If I hadn't felt so envious of you, I never would have fallen under Sulis's spell. She was able to get me because of my envy. It was my strongest motivation, and she used it to trap me. Again, Tavish, will you forgive me?"

Tavish embraced his brother, and the two of

them hugged and slapped each other's backs, but Amber could see that Tomas was crying silently as Tavish spoke his pardon.

"Of course I forgive you. You're my brother, and I'll always be there for you. I'm so, so glad to have you back!"

Amber and Kelsey laughed and clapped and cheered at that. And then the musicians got up and played, and they all joined in on the set dances, even Deirdre, who laughed when the men picked her up to twirl her around instead of linking elbows with her.

Once the dancing was well underway, Tomas took Amber by the hand and led her back to the edge of the cliff, where they stood hand-in-hand watching the sea. It was cloudy as usual, but they could just make out Ireland in the distance over the water, and Amber wondered how soon Mr. Blair would get that motorboat so they could go explore. What a great honeymoon that would make.

Tomas startled her out of her reverie.

"What's on your mind, Mrs. MacGregor?"

For a moment, Amber looked around to see who he was talking to. And then she saw the teasing look on his face and laughed.

"I'm eager to get on with being married, Mr. McGregor."

He kissed her then, a warm loving kiss full of promise, and then turned them back toward the wedding party area.

"It looks like you're not the only one."

Sure enough, Kelsey & Tavish and Sasha &

Seumas were all headed toward the stairs that went down into the underground palace.

Tomas put his arm around Amber's waist and turned them toward the stairs too.

"I think we'd better catch up with them, because I'm not sure they'll wait for us."

Laughing, Amber hustled off arm-in-arm with her husband, toward their future.

Fichead (20)

Amber sat awkwardly on the bed in the room she now shared with Tomas in the trailer, resting her bare foot on a folded pillow so she could paint her toenails dark blue. On her cell speaker she was also talking with Jaelle, their faire friend who had still been with John until six months ago.

"Yeah, the Scottish skies were sunny for once, and we had a beautiful old time wedding on the cliff overlooking the Irish Sea—and then we all high-tailed it back here to the present."

"But no one in the present knew you were married, and no time had passed in order for you to get married in. How did you deal with that?"

Forgetting she was talking on the phone and not in person —or perhaps just accustomed to being flamboyant when she spoke—Amber gestured wildly, and a blob of blue nail polish fell off the brush. Good thing she had put a paper towel down on the pillow. Wait, what was she thinking?

Amber laughed.

Jaelle sounded amused.

"Must be a good story."

Amber grabbed up the paper towel, wadded it, and made a basket into the trashcan. She just barely remembered she still had the brush in her hand before she raised her arms up high and declared a score— and got nail polish who knew where.

"No, no. I was laughing because I splattered some nail polish."

"Huh?"

"It could've gotten on the pillowcase if it weren't for this paper towel, but with the amount Mr. Blair is paying me for helping Emily out with her cataloging system for the dig, I could buy a thousand pillowcases, so what am I worried about?"

They laughed together for a moment, and then Jaelle cleared her throat.

Amber snorted to let her old friend know she'd received the subtle hint to get on with her story.

"Okay, I know you don't want to hear about that. We made our marriage legal two days after we got back to the present. We just flew back home and saw a justice of the peace."

"Aw, that's too bad—"

"No, I wanted it that way. Over and done with as quickly as possible so we could get on with married life, already—"

Jaelle burst into a loud peal of laughter.

Amber growled at her playfully.

"Oh, would you get your mind out of the gutter for once. My family were all there to witness my happiness, and getting married to Tomas was all that really mattered to me. It wasn't about the dress, or the ring, or having to dance to a certain song at a reception, cutting the cake, throwing the bouquet, riding in a limousine, or picking out bridesmaids' dresses. It was about declaring in front of witnesses our intention to spend the rest of our lives together as husband and wife."

To Amber's puzzlement, Jaelle's voice sounded clipped when she spoke next.

"Did you at least get a honeymoon?"

Huh. Where was that coming from?

"Tavish & Kelsey and Seumas & Sasha had plane tickets to Hawaii already, so they were all gone for two weeks. Me and Tomas were bummed we couldn't go along — until Mr. Blair showed up with the motorboat he'd been promising everyone."

Jaelle blew her nose. Maybe she was getting sick. That would explain her tone. A runny nose would make anyone impatient. Yeah, that must be it. She sounded stuffed up when she spoke.

"Wow, cool."

Amber brought the pillow forward a little bit so

it was easier to reach her toes, and then she put down a fresh paper towel and repositioned her foot on it. This time when she dipped the brush back in, she was much more careful to wipe off the glob at the end of it against the bottleneck.

"You can say that again. It has a cabin and everything, and when he heard we just got married, he let us take it over to Ireland for a week, all by ourselves. We docked at a different port every night and went sight-seeing every day, not to mention all the pub crawling we did. Couldn't have planned a better honeymoon if I tried. —And like I said before, on Tuesday we're headed 'down unda' to Australia to learn the business-end of the faire. When I hear myself say that, I just can't believe it. I get Tomas in the fair in Australia and Dall and Emily back as my friends... All my dreams are coming true!"

Jaelle had been quiet longer than usual.

Guilt grabbed Amber's heart and yanked on it till it hurt.

"Listen to me, going on about how happy Tomas and I are. How are you doing? I can't believe you and John defied his parents, let alone broke up after seven years of defiance together. Really, how are you doing?"

Jaelle sniffled.

"Thanks for shutting up about you and Tomas. Now shut up about me and John." She laughed a little.

Amber laughed a little, too.

"Sorry. That was really stupid of me. All of it. What kind of friend am I?"

"No, I get it. And I'm really happy for you. You and Tomas are both great people, and I know how in love you are. And I'm one of the few who know why you were apart these past seven years. I know you never really broke up, how Dall and Emily dropped a bomb on him and Tavish on their eighteenth birthday and he disappeared from your life to protect you. Dall and Emily thought they were doing the right thing, you know, not telling him until then. You do know that, right? Because I don't hate them, and you shouldn't either."

"I don't hate them. I know it's not their fault. He told me the story about their ancestor with a gambling problem — uh oh, I hope I'm not saying something you don't already know." She laughed her exaggerated nervous laugh.

"Yeah, that story. I bet it was a lot easier for you to believe than it was for me, after what you just went through. I'm having trouble believing your story, and I've known the gambling story for seven years now." Jaelle laughed again, and this time there was actually joy in it.

"Heh," said Amber, "I wouldn't believe my story if I hadn't lived it, so I know what you mean. But here we are talking about me again. I really want to know if you're okay, and if there's anything I can do to help you. I'm not even above going over and giving John a piece of my mind, if that will help."

Jaelle cleared her throat.

"About that."

"What?"

"Well, has Tomas told you how he's related to John?"

"Huh? We've always known."

"Okay, we always thought we knew, but Amber, John's dad isn't just some random part of Dall's fifteenth century MacGregor clan. He's Tomas and Tavish's brother."

"Nuh uh! He can't be. He's Dall's same age."

"Right, but now you know this is a time-traveling family."

"So?"

"So Dall was born in the early 1500s. He got married when he was young and had three children: Peadar, Peigi, and Dombnall. His wife died when they were twenty three. Then Dall turned twenty five and started his servitude with the druids. They picked Emily out for him among some others and brought her and the others back to his time for him to bond with her. When she got back to her own time, she didn't remember that. They had cursed her so that she wouldn't remember time travel unless she joined with him—"

Amber cut in.

"Get to the point already. What does that have to do with John's dad Peadar?"

"I'm getting to that. Just listen."

"Okay, but get to it faster."

"Very funny. So anyway, Dall and Emily got together, right, and then they started experimenting with time travel. They had a lot more freedom to time travel than John and Tavish do, because they had an app on their cell phone that enabled them to go to any time and any place where a loved one was—"

Amber gasped.

"You're kidding."

Jaelle laughed.

"You and Tomas sure haven't been doing very much talking."

Amber laughed too.

"Shut up. Yeah, we're a married couple who should know all these things about each other, but we only just now got back together. There hasn't been time to talk about everything."

"Uh huh. So anyway, Dall and Emily could go to any time or place where one of their loved ones was. The druids had Tavish living mostly in our time, but Emily told Dall about how the MacGregor name would soon be outlawed back in his time. So they sought out his son Peadar when he was twenty-five, to make sure he was okay. Vange went with them, and as soon as she met Peadar — well, you know how in love those two are."

There was a scraping noise on Jaelle's end of the line.

"What was that?"

"Oh sorry. I told you John let me keep his house after he broke off our engagement, right?"

"Yeah, you did. And I have to admit, that was really nice of him. Most guys wouldn't even let you keep the ring."

Jaelle snorted a laugh.

"It's not like he's still paying the rent. Anyway, I'm going through the boxes of junk he left in the basement, and some of this stuff is really cool. Here, I'll take a picture of this helmet I just found so you can see."

Amber waited, and then she got a text with a picture. The helmet was really dark, like an iron skillet.

"Wow, that is cool."

"Isn't it? Here, I'm going into video chat to try it on so you can see."

Amber laughed.

"Okay."

There was a pause as Jaelle set the phone down and ran around in front of the camera holding the helmet.

"Are you watching? I can't tell."

"Yeah, I can see you."

Jaelle held the helmet over her head.

"Here goes."

Amber thought this whole idea of trying on the helmet was silly, but Jaelle was hurting inside from losing John, even though she tried to play it off like she wasn't. So Amber humored her. She felt terrible about going on and on about herself and Tomas.

But she soon forgot all about those worries.

And then some.

Because as soon as Jaelle put the helmet on...

She disappeared.

Amber screamed.

Kelsey came running in.

"What's the matter? You look like you've seen a ghost — and I certainly hope you haven't discovered that ghosts are real. Please tell me they aren't." Her friend had been smiling up to that point, but now her face grew serious. "Wow, something's really spooked you. What is it?"

Too shocked to even speak, Amber pushed play on the video of the call and handed her phone to Kelsey.

Kelsey gasped.

"Well, at least we'll be able to see it in her dreams."

"Huh? See what?"

"That was a Roman helmet Jaelle put on, from the period when they were building Hadrian's Wall."

Amber made a sour face.

"I'm not excited about the Romans."

Kelsey's face had cracked into a huge grin.

"Me neither, but the Romans built that wall to keep out of England the people they called savages."

"And?"

"And Jaelle just went back to the time of the Celts."

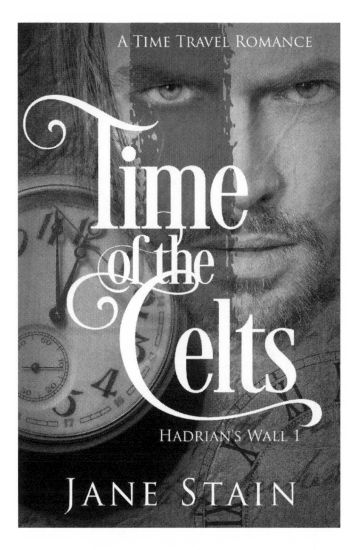

A TIME TRAVEL ROMANCE

Time of the Celts

HADRIAN'S WALL 1

JANE STAIN

Get the next book at Amazon.com!

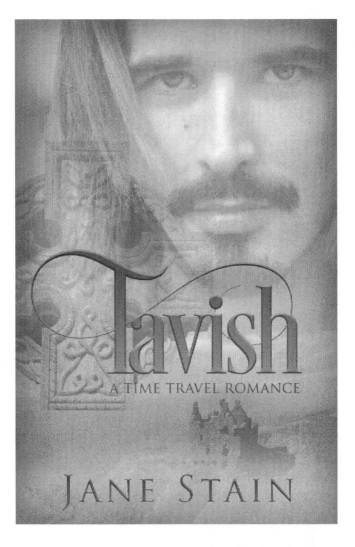

Get the first book
in the Dunskey Castle Series
at Amazon.com!

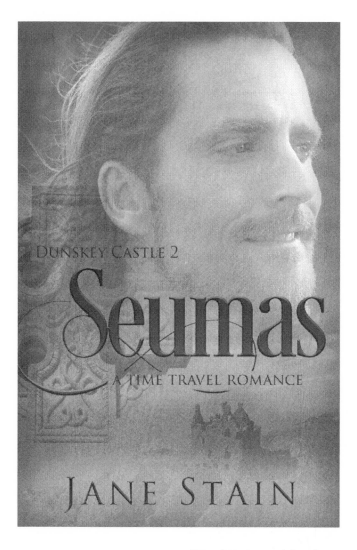

Get the second book
in the Dunskey Castle Series
at Amazon.com!

JANE STAIN

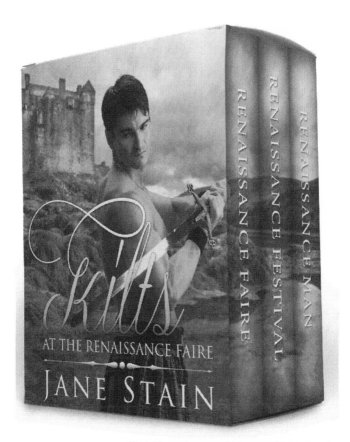

Get the story of Tomas's parents
At Amazon.com!
The moment budding drama teacher Emily Shaw lays
eyes on handsome highlander Dall MacGregor, she
wants to ... have his babies. But then she's afraid
she'll never see him again. The faire people seem
bent on keeping the two of them from talking privately.
But over the summer, she talks her way into time
traveling with him to 1540.

ABOUT THE AUTHOR

Jane Stain is a pen name for
Cherise Kelley.

Sign up for her newsletter and get
sneak previews of upcoming books!

janestain.com

JANE STAIN